Contents

Mary Arrigan

seascape with barber's harp

Illustrated by Terry Myler

THE CHILDREN'S PRESS

To my husband
Emmet
with love

First published 1997 by
The Children's Press
an imprint of Anvil Books
45 Palmerston Road, Dublin 6

S345,526   2 4 6 5 3 1

© Text Mary Arrigan 1997
© Illustrations The Children's Press

ISBN 1 901737 02 0

Typeset by Computertype Limited
Printed by Colour Books Limited

1

Off to Baltimore

My mother should have known better than to rush towards me when I was trying out my new online skates.

'It's from Lond...' she began, just before both of us collapsed into the viburnum bush.

'Mam!' I cried, as she lay sprawled on her back. 'Speak to me! I don't want to be an orphan!'

She growled something she shouldn't have said in front of her only child and pulled herself up. 'This letter,' she held a blue envelope in front of me. 'It's from London.'

'So?' I said, spitting on my grazed knee and wiping away the trace of blood. I should have worn the knee-guards, but they make my legs look shorter. One has one's pride.

'For you, Maeve,' she said impatiently. 'A letter from London for you.'

'Wow! Who's it from?'

She shook her head. 'I didn't read it. I don't read other people's letters.'

But I knew from the way she said it that the letter must have been burning a hole in her mind all morning.

'Aren't you going to read it?' she asked as I put it in the back pocket of my shorts.

'Maybe later,' I called as I glided back down to the pavement. Of course I was dying to read it, but I wanted Mam to suffer. Power, you see, corrupts even the sweetest of us.

I waited until I'd skated past the corner before doing my nifty heel-stop. It didn't quite come off, but luckily there was a brick wall to stop me. I spent a few moments examining the handwriting on the envelope before tearing it open.

'Good grief, it's from Jamie!' I exclaimed out loud. 'Good old Jamie. He's invited me to Baltimore.'

Jamie Stephenson is a good friend. He's what you'd call upmarket but, aside from the posh accent which he can't help because he grew up with it, he isn't in the least bit priggish. At least not now. Not since he met me. Baltimore! Mega magic! I couldn't wait to get home to tell Mam. She'd gone back to where she was building a rockery at the bottom of the garden.

'I've been invited to Baltimore,' I shouted from the edge of the lawn. 'Jamie has invited me to Baltimore. He's spending the last couple of weeks of the summer there with his folks. Can I go?'

Now it was Mam's turn to show power. She took off the heavy gloves she used to protect her hands from the rough stones and came towards me with annoying slowness. I handed her the letter and sat down to undo my skates.

'Can I go?' I asked again. She finished reading the letter and handed it back to me.

'I don't see why not,' she said. 'It will be a nice end to the summer for you.'

My jaw bounced off my chest. She was agreeing, just like that. Not even a hint of doubt. She must have hit her head in that tumble.

'But ... can we afford it?' I muttered. 'The fare and all that. Can we afford it?'

Mam looked at me quizzically. 'Won't be all that dear,' she said. 'You'll get half fare on the train.'

'Train? Mam, what are you saying? This is *Baltimore*

we're talking about. This is a molto biggo journey. We're talking jumbo jets here. You know, big bird flying in the sky...'

Mam gave me that look again. 'Maeve, honey, read the letter again. Say each word out loud. The Baltimore you're invited to is in West Cork, not the one in America.'

'Huh?' I looked at the letter. Sure enough I'd skipped the last bit in my excitement. 'West Cork! That's ...that's right down in the middle of nowhere. It's miles away.'

'It's a bit closer than the States,' laughed Mam. 'And you were all for going *there*.'

'That's different,' I growled. 'America's different. West Cork! I'd be brain dead in a day.'

Which wasn't quite true, of course. You don't get brain dead around people like Jamie. I'd first met Jamie when I was staying with my cousin Leo and his folks in the midlands. Jamie was staying at his grandfather's large estate near Leo's house. The three of us had got caught up in a scam that involved ancient artifacts being shipped out of the country, and we ended up being national heroes. No, life would not be boring with Jamie around. Besides which he'd grown into a pretty okay looker.

'I suppose Leo will be going too,' said Mam, putting on the heavy-duty gloves again.

'What?'

'Leo. I expect Jamie will have asked him too.'

'Oh, rats!' I exclaimed. I didn't want a nerdy eleven-year-old cramping my style.

Mam shook her head. 'Where's your good nature?' she sighed as she began heaving the big stones into her rockery. You don't hang around disturbed mothers who are wielding heavy rocks, so I slunk away in my stock-inged feet.

Up in my room I sat on my bed and thought about seeing Jamie again. Strange. Sometimes it felt like he was a brother, other times he was like Romeo to my Juliet, Rhett Butler to my Scarlett O'Hara, Othello to my Cleopatra.

I could feel a poem coming on, so I fished out my very secret folder from under a pile of tee-shirts. My poetry collection was getting quite thick. Soon I'd have enough to send to some lucky publisher who'd thank his stars for the day that my volume, *Poems by Maeve Morris*, landed on his desk. I already had the spot on the mantelpiece picked out for the Nobel Prize for Poetry. I took out my special pink poetry biro and began to write. I was getting good at this. When you have truly natural talent like I have, the words just flow.

Love in the Wilderness

By Maeve Morris

I'm going to see my love in Cork.
He's really cool and not a dork.
For me it would be simply grand
If he would kiss my fragile hand.
And so I'll wend through bog and shore
To see his groovy face once more.

Later that day Leo rang. He was practically hopping into the phone with excitement.

'Sailing!' he shrieked. 'Jamie says that we can all go sailing. His folks own a yacht and we'll get to ride in it.'

Sailing? There had been no mention of sailing in my letter. Maybe Jamie had wanted to surprise me. Just as well I now knew in advance, so that my face wouldn't register horrified panic at the mention of sailing. Rolling over deep water in a glorified tub which is guided by a sheet on a pole is not my idea of fun.

At supper time, Dad grinned as he passed me the tomato ketchup.

'So, our Maeve is off to fraternise with people of the yachting persuasion. That'll knock the wind out of your tough feminist sails,' he chortled at his own awful pun. 'Surviving on the water cuts through all that equality hoo-ha. Everyone has to do their bit. You'll be wishing for the days when a lady just had to sit back and let others do the work.'

'Terrible joke, Dad,' I muttered. Dad was a kid in the sixties and got stuck in a time warp. He thinks that women are still fighting for equality and all that stuff. 'The word feminist is old hat now. You should join the human race and get a life.'

He laughed again and made some rude sea-sick gestures. Makes you wonder how a man like that could produce a sensitive poet like me.

Then he suddenly got that serious concerned-parent look on his face. 'On no account are you to board any boat of any kind unless there's an experienced adult with you,' he said. 'Remember, the sea has no mercy. One slip and you're a goner.'

'Dad,' I said. 'In the first place I've no particular interest in bobbing about in boring old water in a boring old tug. I'll be finding better things to do. In the second place, if I *do* get into one of those things I'll need a captain, crew and several life-guards with me. Do you take me for a total nerd? Do you think I'm going to sail single-handed across the Atlantic?'

Mam stopped buttering her bread and leaned towards

me. 'Listen to your father,' she said. 'It's very important that you keep his warning right up there in that scattered brain of yours. Only sail with adults who know and respect the sea.'

'I know, I know,' I muttered. What did they take me for? I really hate it when they give me their squirmingly meaningful advice.

'And life-jackets,' went on Dad. 'Proper life-jackets at all times. Never set foot in a boat unless you have a fastened life-jacket on you.'

'Are you listening, Maeve?' put in Mam. 'We're very serious.'

'I hear you,' I replied. 'I'll wear a parachute as well if it makes you happy.'

'Maeve!' snapped Mam, waving her buttery knife at me.

'Yes, yes,' I said. 'I hear and obey, O honourable parents. Adult and life-jacket. Got it.'

Mam looked me up and down when I got up to get some ice-cream from the freezer. I knew what was on her mind.

'Don't even think it, Mam,' I said. 'These clothes are just perfect.'

'Maybe just a couple of nice summer dresses...' she began. 'You'll be mixing with nice people...'

I put my hands over my ears. 'Mam! I'm going to a place where there's wilderness on one side and salty water on the other. Trainers and jeans are just right. I refuse to wear dresses.'

She gave another one of her exasperated sighs and shook her head.

'No nice pretty frock to impress Jamie?' put in Dad. Had he been reading my poetry? No, my verses would be much too classy for him. 'Careful, Maeve, he might go and fall for some shimmering sailing type down there in West Cork.'

That was the last straw. 'I'm going to bed,' I said. 'This is the most disfin ... disfunch...'

'I think dysfunctional is the word you're floundering for, honeybun,' said Dad.

'Yeah, well.'

They were both laughing when I flounced out of the room.

Still, I mused, as I took a critical look at myself in the mirror, it might not be any harm to tame my Brillo-type hair and pick up a few trendy tops that would do justice to my blue eyes. I practised opening my eyes really wide, like I'd seen Kate Winslet do in *Sense and Sensibility*. That made me look really interesting.

'Okay, Jamie and West Cork,' I muttered just before I turned out the lamp. 'I'm ready for you.'

2

The First Disaster

Leo was the only passenger to get on at Ballybrophy, a tiny station on the Dublin to Cork line. It was the nearest station to his town, Kildioma. He looked lost sitting there with his enormous rucksack. His face lit up when he saw me waving to him. For an eleven-year-old Leo is fairly tolerable. A bit of a knowall who presses his nose into nerdy books and surfs the internet with like-minded cyberfreaks, but when you get him out in the fresh air he's almost human.

'Hi, you,' I said when he'd struggled down to where I was sitting. 'Imagine this whole train had to stop just to pick up a little prat like you.'

He grinned with big teeth that his face hadn't caught up with yet.

'Hi, yourself. Ha!' He pointed to my head. 'What have you done to your hair? You look like a lavatory brush.'

I narrowed my eyes threateningly. 'Watch it, sunshine,' I said. 'Don't mess with your superiors.'

But he was right about the hair. I'd let Mam take me to her own pre-historic hairdresser and the result was disastrous. I'd been so busy reading *Hello!* magazine that I hadn't noticed the big chunks of hair that the scissor-happy old bat had chopped off. I'd sworn to become either a nun or a muslim, or join any sect that involved women's heads being covered, just until it grew again.

'You look really pretty,' Mam had said when I crawled home. 'It shows off your long neck.'

'That's all I need,' I'd said. 'To be told I look like a

14

cruddy giraffe. I can't go to Baltimore looking like this.'

'Believe me, sweetheart, you look great,' Mam had insisted. 'Elegant and sophisticated.'

And, now that I'd almost convinced myself that I really had a beautiful, elegant neck like Celine Dion, this rotten kid was driving me right back to freakdom.

'Where are your folks?' I asked, changing the subject. 'How come they left you here alone in this deserted dive to frighten the natives?'

Leo's mother, Brid, is my mam's sister. After Leo's dad died, she married Jim. He owns a vegetarian restaurant in the town of Kildioma. They live in a cottage outside the town and they grow their own vegetables. Not my kind of lifestyle, but they're really off-beat and fun to be with. When he found some old photos of his dad, Leo went through a bad patch with Jim. Even though he didn't really remember his dad, he resented Jim for taking his place. However, when we'd been in danger over that ancient artifacts scam, Jim and Leo had become really close again.

'They had to get back,' Leo said, squashing in beside his rucksack on the seat opposite. 'Restaurant's busy for the summer and Mam is helping Jim. They had to go and collect the babysitter for Miriam.'

Miriam is Leo's baby half-sister. I often envied him that. But then, being an only child brings its own privileges – like having nobody to mess about with your stuff and being fairly confident that you'll get what you want.

'Are you excited, Maeve?' asked Leo, offering me some hairy mints from his pocket.

'Excited? Nah,' I said with feigned boredom. 'I expect West Cork will be all line-dancing and sawdust pubs.'

'So, why are you coming then?' Leo said with a scowl. 'If it's so awful why did you agree to come? You'll probably spoil everything on Jamie and me with your long face and ...'

'I will not,' I retorted. 'What long face? Do you see a long face? Only for me you two would have no fun at all.'

We sank into an unfriendly silence. Leo took out a puzzle book and I gazed at the passing fields. Long face indeed! Little prat. *He* was the one who'd spoil it all.

THE INTERLOPER
A 19th-century love poem

By Maeve Morris

The lass's heart beat in her breast
On seeing her lover's manly chest.
'I love you, dearest,' he confessed.
'Of all the maidens, you're the best.'
But just before she could reply,
Her stupid cousin wandered by.
'Oh hell,' she said, with tearful eye.
'That kid is just a rotten spy.
Forgive me, dear, for I must fly.'

The hypnotic clickety-clack of the train lulled me into a deep sleep. Next thing I knew Leo was shaking me.

'Get off,' I muttered. 'What do you want?'

'We're here,' he said, grabbing his big rucksack.

'Already?' I couldn't believe it. 'Surely a journey down to the bottom of Ireland takes longer than that?'

Leo grinned. 'You've been asleep for most of it. Thank goodness,' he added spitefully.

'So this is Cork,' I said as we spilled out on to the platform. 'It's ... it's a big city.'

'And what did you expect?' asked Leo scornfully.

'Thatched cottages and piggy-wiggies?'

'Don't be such a smart-ass,' I retorted. 'I just didn't think it would be so big, that's all.'

'You Dubs are all the same,' said Leo. 'You think everything outside your stupid city is wild country, whereas in fact...'

'Oh, give over,' I said crossly. The long sleep had left me feeling less than wonderful. 'I have to get to the loo before we get the bus to Skibbereen – or whatever it's called.'

'Hurry up then,' said Leo. 'It leaves in ten minutes.'

My main reason for going to the loo was, of course, to make sure I'd look fantastic for meeting Jamie. Maybe he wouldn't notice the hair if I tousled it up a bit. Maybe he'd be so transfixed by the elegant neck that his eyes would skip the hair. There, that wasn't too bad. I practised the wide-eyed look and smoothed the creases out of my new red shirt. It had cost a bomb, but even

Mam had to agree that it was the coolest. Dad had said I'd knock them dead in West Cork. I was happy enough with the way I looked.

The bus was pretty packed, so we had to put our luggage in the boot.

'Are they all going to Skibbereen?' I whispered to Leo. 'What's bringing them to a small town like that...?'

'There you go again. Give it a rest, Maeve.'

'Just asking. No harm in asking,' I said.

What happened next will haunt me for the rest of my life. Put it down to the queasy feeling after sleeping on the train, or the two packets of crisps I'd eaten, or the twisting route along the road from Cork to Skibbereen, but my stomach gave a sudden lurch. Voices became distant and disembodied and everything seemed to fade.

'Leo...' I began. He'd just turned to look at me when I threw up, all over the new red shirt that was supposed to impress Jamie to bits.

'Oh, yecchhh,' cried Leo, leaning away from me.

I stared in disbelief at the mess down my front. It couldn't have happened. Please let this be a bad dream.

'Oh, Maeve,' said Leo. He fished a hanky out of his pocket and handed it to me. Fat lot of good that did.

'What will I do?' I cried in panic. 'Jamie and his mother will be waiting at the bus stop. Jeez, Leo, I can't meet them looking like this!'

Leo looked perplexed. 'Can't you take it off?' he said. 'Change into something else.'

'My blasted rucksack is in the blasted boot!' I moaned.

By now people were looking at me. A stout lady opposite handed me a wodge of tissues.

'There now, dear,' she clucked. 'That can happen when you're not used to travel.'

Of course I'm used to travel, I wanted to shout. *I travel by Dart and bus every day of my life in Dublin.* But I nodded and thanked her. Someone else handed me a bottle of water. I did my best, but my shirt was ruined.

Leo was standing in the aisle. 'Come and sit down,' I hissed. 'Everyone's looking.'

'I will not,' he replied.

'What will I do?' I moaned again. 'I'll stay on the bus. You can tell them I didn't come. Tell them that ...tell them anything you like. I'll just lie low until the bus turns back and I'll go home.'

'Don't be daft, Maeve,' said Leo. 'Look,' he leaned towards me gingerly. 'I'll walk out ahead of you and keep you hidden. When we get to their place you can scarper to the bathroom and clean yourself up.'

'But they'll notice. How could they not notice?'

Leo shrugged. 'We'll sit in the back and keep the windows open. Come on, it'll be all right.'

I looked at him with some doubt. 'And you'll stay in front of me all the time?'

He nodded. 'I promise. Don't worry. It'll be all right.'

'Well, okay then. If you're sure...'

'I am. You'll be fine. Look, we're here.'

'Oh, God,' I groaned. Outside, on the pavement, Jamie and a classy looking woman who was probably his mother were looking at the disembarking passengers.

'Wait, Leo,' I cried. 'I can't do this.'

But Leo was already halfway down the aisle. He waited for me to catch up. 'Now,' he said. 'Stay right behind me and everything will be fine.'

I took a deep breath and followed him down the steps.

3

A Bad Start

'There they are!' shouted Jamie, rushing towards us. I grabbed the back of Leo's jumper to keep him near me.

'Don't worry,' he whispered.

'Hi, Jamie,' I called, with forced cheerfulness. 'Just hold on there while we get our stuff from the boot.' That way I could clutch my rucksack and hide the mess.

'I'll take that,' he replied, still coming towards us.

The driver had opened the boot and was pulling the contents on to the pavement. Leo and I walked like Siamese twins. By the time we got to the luggage, Jamie was in front of us, grinning. His grin froze when Leo bent down to retrieve his rucksack, exposing the stain on my red shirt – the shirt that was supposed to impress.

Even under such horrendous conditions, my razor-sharp mind was at work.

'There was a woman on the train,' I began. 'She had a heart attack and I went to help her. She threw up on me, but I didn't mind. You don't think of yourself at times like that...'

By now the elegant woman was beside us. She had fair hair, like Jamie's, cut into a fashionable bob. She wore white jeans and a blue and white striped sweatshirt. Her tanned face made her teeth seem even whiter as she smiled at us. I felt more miserable than ever.

'Mum, this is Leo,' said Jamie. Leo reached out and shook Mrs Stephenson's hand, again leaving me exposed. I was about to launch into my heart-attack story again, but Jamie interrupted. 'And this is Maeve,' he continued.

'She got sick,' put in Leo. He looked at me and smiled. 'See?' he said. 'Nobody minds.'

The three of them looked at me for what seemed like forever. I felt like one of those lepers who used to ring a bell and cry 'Unclean, unclean'.

'You poor child,' said Jamie's mother, instinctively withdrawing the hand she was offering. It was an awkward moment – I shuffled and blushed, Jamie's mouth opened and shut like the gob of a sick fish, while Leo shifted uneasily from one foot to the other. 'We must get you home and cleaned up,' she continued. 'Would you like anything? A cup of tea? Glass of water?'

I gulped and shook my head. This was a brilliant start. Really brilliant. Just before we got into the car, I pinched Leo really hard. 'You creep,' I hissed. 'You could have gone along with the heart thing.'

'Ouch! Don't be daft, Maeve. Who'd believe a yarn like that? Get real. See? It's no big deal.'

Still, he sat as far away from me as possible as we headed out of Skibbereen towards Baltimore.

'Let me know if you're feeling any way unwell,' said Jamie's mother, discreetly letting down her window. 'I'll stop anywhere you want me to.'

Now I felt more like a leper than ever. A grotesque, begging leper with extra scabs and bad hair.

THE BEAUTIFUL BEGGAR GIRL

By Maeve Morris

They passed her by, that heartless crew,
And never saw her eyes so blue.
She begged for food, perhaps some dosh,
But they were cruel and much too posh.

S345,520

Leo oohhed and aahhed all the way to Baltimore. As Leo would, of course.

'Look, Maeve,' he'd enthuse. 'Look, you can see the sea.' Or, 'Look, Maeve, masses of boats.'

It all passed over my head; I was much too miserable for scenery. I mostly kept my head down in the hope that nobody would notice I existed. But I must admit I was really impressed when we drove up a private lane to the most wonderful house I've ever seen. It was all wood and glass, the sort you'd see in glossy magazines. There was a front balcony that looked right out to the sea.

'Wow!' I whispered, awestruck.

'That's Mount Gabriel over there,' said Jamie, pointing across the water. 'And Sherkin Island to the left...'

'Jamie, will you let the unfortunate girl change out of her soiled clothes before you start your guided tour.'

'Poor child!' 'Unfortunate girl!' – I'd really hit zilch in this lady's esteem. She turned to me and held out her hand purposefully, as if to make up for her earlier *faux pas*. 'Come along, dear. Let's get you sorted out.'

I wiped my hand on a clean part of my jeans before taking hers and following her up a spiral stairs and into a big sunny room. A low bed with a big blue and yellow patterned duvet was tucked into a corner. Bright wall-hangings adorned the timber walls. There were colourful rugs on the floor. The huge window looked out on to the scene that Jamie had been pointing out.

I was gobsmacked. 'Is this ... is this my room?' I was almost afraid to ask in case she said no.

She smiled. 'All yours,' she said. 'The boys are sharing a room across the landing. Now, leave your rucksack down and I'll show you the bathroom.'

That was equally impressive – all wood and rugs and

matching towels. It smelled like the Body Shop and had shelves of interesting looking lotions and potions.

'No frosted glass,' I said, looking at the bay through another huge window.

Jamie's mother laughed. 'No, indeed. You're not in ...' she broke off. What had she been about to say? I wondered. I bristled slightly. *I know she's Jamie's mum*, I thought. *But there's something less than warm and mumsy about her. More your average frozen haddock.*

'It's nice to look out as you bathe,' she added quickly. 'And don't worry. Unless there's some fisherman out there with extra powerful binoculars, no one will see your ablutions.'

Still, later on, I stuck a towel across part of the window while I took my shower, just in case. I looked at my body and wondered whereabouts on my anatomy my ablutions were. It was good to feel clean. I helped myself to the scented talc and lotions. Now I could start over again, this time smelling of magnolia and lavender.

Leo and Jamie were helping to set the table when I came downstairs. The living area was a huge open-plan affair. The front looked over the bay, the back was a compact kitchen. There were long window seats and lots of sofas scattered about. It was a lotto dreamer's ideal home. A delicious smell of something garlicky wafted from the cooker. In spite of my mishap I was starving.

'Just in time,' said Jamie's mum, carrying a casserole to the table. 'And here comes the hungry sailor.'

We all looked up as a tall tanned man wearing yellow oilskins breezed in – an old-guy version of Jamie. He was in the British army – some high-ranking bod in the UN Jamie had told us. You'd have known he was in the army because his arms and legs had a disciplined way of moving, if you know what I mean. His intelligent face showed him to be the type who'd do hard crosswords and know about boring stuff like politics and income tax.

'So, the gang's all here,' he said, peeling off the oilskins and hanging them in a niche behind the door.

Jamie introduced us. I was glad he hadn't been around to see me earlier. Now, maybe someone would notice my elegant neck. We sat down at the big table and Jamie's dad began to ladle out the stew.

'Maeve,' said Jamie's mum, coming towards me with a plate. 'I've done you a poached egg and toast. I figured it would be lighter on your stomach.' She turned to her husband. 'Poor child was sick on the bus,' she explained.

They all turned to look at me and I died a death. Would I never be allowed to forget that stupid incident?

'I'm all right,' I muttered. 'It was nothing...'

'Just embarrassing,' said Leo. 'Mega embarrassing.'

I screwed up my eyes, but he didn't notice. Later, I promised myself. I'll strangle him later.

4

The Dark Spanish Stranger

After tea, Jamie took us down to the small shingle beach in front of the house. There was a 'Private' notice stuck in the ground.

'Private?' I asked.

Jamie laughed. 'Yeah. Came with the house.'

'Who owns the house?' Leo asked. 'Are you renting it?'

'No,' replied Jamie. 'It belongs to friends of my parents – people they go sailing with. It's a sort of swap really. Mum and Dad have given them the use of our holiday house down near Marseilles.'

Neither Leo or I said anything. We were too awestruck.

'That's in Provence,' added Jamie, mistaking our deafening silence for ignorance.

'I know that,' I retorted. 'We're not that thick that we don't know where Marseilles is.'

'Where is it then?' asked Leo with a malicious grin. I narrowed my eyes and mouthed the words 'drop dead' at him.

'It's down,' (Jamie had used that word, so it must be in the south), 'down near, you know...'

'Just around the corner from the Cote d'Azur,' put in Jamie.

'Just what I was about to say,' I went on. 'Down near the the... Coat du Jour.'

'You were in your eye going to say that,' laughed Leo. 'You haven't the foggiest.'

'Cool it, you two,' said Jamie, picking up a smooth pebble and skimming it across the water. I was surprised to see that he was annoyed. Normally he'd laugh at our silly rowing.

There was a dinghy moored to a big iron ring on the shingle beach. It had an outboard motor on the back. 'That's the dinghy that takes us across to the yacht,' went on Jamie. He pointed to where lots of yachts were rocking gently in the evening light. Their high masts were reflected in the water. Dangerous looking things. There was no way I was going to board one of those. No siree.

'Which one's yours?' asked Leo.

'That one with "Cordelia Lyn" written on it.'

'Cordelia Lyn?' I said.

Jamie grinned. 'That's Mum's name. It was an anniversary present. '

I smiled a satisfied smile to myself. Cordelia Lyn! I might have made a show of myself by throwing up on a bus. But that was over and done with. Jamie's mum would have to carry a daft name like Cordelia Lyn for the rest of her life.

'Who owns that great big one that's moored farther out than all the others?' asked Leo.

'I don't know,' replied Jamie. 'It's a beaut, isn't it? I haven't seen such a super yacht in years. I wonder who owns it.'

They were looking out beyond the bay, to where this big yacht with several masts was floating majestically on the water.

'Pity I didn't bring my binoculars,' went on Jamie. 'I'd like to identify that vessel.'

'Maybe they don't want to be identified,' I said. 'Maybe they just want a quiet holiday out there on the water, away from people gaping at them through binoculars. They could be pop stars looking for peace and quiet.'

Jamie gave me a mock scathing look. 'You don't know much about sailing etiquette, Maeve,' he said. 'It's polite when you sail into a harbour to fly your colours and declare yourself...'

'What a load of old baloney,' I scoffed.

Jamie laughed. 'Maybe you're right,' he said.

'Can we have a ride in the dinghy?' Leo was asking.

'No!' I exclaimed. 'I mean, it's late. Look, the sun is going down. Anyway...' I added, then stopped.

'Anyway what?' said Leo.

I wished he hadn't asked. 'Anyway, we were warned not to go out in boats without an adult,' I mumbled, feeling totally childish. 'An adult and life-jackets. Dad and Mam warned me.'

'Pah!' scoffed Leo. 'What they meant was not to go in a boat without someone who knows all about the sea. You know all about the sea, don't you, Jamie?'

But, mercifully, Jamie was shaking his head. 'Maeve's right,' he said. 'It's getting a bit late. By the time we'd go back for the life-jackets it would be dusk. Tomorrow. We'll go for a row tomorrow.'

'Oh, wow!' exclaimed Leo.

'Come on,' continued Jamie.'Let's go down to the village and see if there's any action.'

'Now that's my kind of language,' I laughed, relieved that the watery moment had been put off.

We wandered down the hill into Baltimore.It looked like a setting from an old seafaring movie, nestling there at the bottom of the hill. Apart from the traffic, I shouldn't think it had changed much in years and years. The lights from the boats danced on the water and there was lots of laughter and chatter on the pavement that overlooked the harbour.

'Look at that view!' cried Leo.

'I'm looking, I'm looking,' I said. But my view was different from Leo's. I was looking at the cool bunches of people sitting around. Deadly interesting people, all tans and teeth and sailing-type gear. This was my scene.

'Grab a seat,' said Jamie, pointing to big barrels with seats around them outside a pub called Bushe's. 'I'll get us some Coke.'

'Cripes, Maeve, isn't this just the grooviest thing?' said Leo eagerly as he hoisted himself on to one of the stools. 'Look at all these people. I'll bet they've been to all sorts of exotic places in their boats.'

'Yachts,' I said.

'What?'

'They're called yachts. Don't show your ignorance by calling them boats.'

'What do you know?' muttered Leo.

'Just try to look like you're used to all this,' I whispered. 'We don't want people to think that we're a couple of yobbos.'

'Oh, oh,' said Leo as Jamie came back with three glasses of Coke. 'Watch out, Jamie. Maeve is in her "make an impression" mood.'

'I am not,' I retorted.

'Yes you are.' Leo was grinning like a ventriloquist's dummy. 'You want to make like you're part of this.' He raised his voice. 'And you've never been in anything bigger than a rickety row-boat on the river at Granny's.'

'Wimp,' I hissed.

'For crying out loud!' exclaimed Jamie. 'Can't you two try being civil? Bickering's boring.'

Leo and I were shocked into scowling an unwilling truce at one another. This wasn't like Jamie. Tetchiness wasn't high on his list of characteristics. I looked at him to see if he'd grin, but he didn't. Maybe it was a touch of anti-climax, I reasoned. Sometimes, when you look forward to something really intensely, it ends up a bit less than you'd expected. Maybe Jamie had been really intense about our coming and, now we were here, we didn't measure up. Not to worry, I'd sort him out with subtlety and charm.

'So, what's got up your nose?' I asked him.

'Nothing,' he replied. 'Just...just don't carry on. You and Leo, don't be bickering.'

Leo glanced at me and shrugged. I shrugged back, but neither of us said anything.

More people were coming up from the harbour now. In McCarthy's pub on the corner, a folk group had started up. Apart from my wart of a cousin, this was absolutely perfect. I took a deep breath to savour it all. The music, the water, the chatter, the colourful people – it was all thrillingly hypnotic.

'Excuse me, do you mind if we sit here?' A soft, foreign-accented voice broke across my trance. I turned to see the most amazing eyes looking at me. The owner was about nineteen, with a darker than dark tan, black hair pulled back into a neat ponytail, and a face to die for.

I tried to speak, but could only manage a strangled croak.

'May we sit here?' he asked again.

'Yeah, sure,' said Jamie. 'Plenty of room.'

'It *is* crowded, isn't it?' went on the newcomer.

'Just coming up to the end of the sailing season,' replied Jamie chattily. 'In two weeks or so it will have eased off.'

'Are you a sailor?' asked Leo. 'Have you a boat...' he glanced hastily at me, 'I mean a yacht?'

The man laughed. 'No,' he replied, 'I cycle. I'm cycling around West Cork.'

'Where are you from?' went on Leo. There are times when he has his uses. Asking questions of cool strangers is one of them.

'Spain,' he was told. 'I am from Spain. Have you ever been to Spain?'

Leo shook his head.

'Yes,' put in Jamie. 'Many times.'

I nodded so that the hunk would think my answer was the same as Jamie's. Then the two of them set to talking about places like Barcelona and Costa Whatsit. I just watched, moonstruck. I bet he's dead romantic, I thought. And he lives on an olive ranch and has a mother called Consuela or Conchita or something, and a house with lots of arches surrounded by those spiky trees you see in hot countries.

THE DARK SPANISH STRANGER

By Maeve Morris

'Twas by the sea she met her Don,
The king of olive oil.
He took her in his swarthy arms,
All muscular from toil.
'Your neck,' he said, 'is like a swan's,
That floats upon the pool.
You look so deadly elegant
So charming and so cool.'

'Hello.' Another voice broke across my poetic musing. I turned to see a smiling girl with long black hair tied back with a red scarf. She was carrying two glasses of Guinness which she plonked on the barrel in front of us, and then climbed on to the other vacant stool.

Wouldn't you know it! Just when I was ready to join the conversation with some scintillating remarks, a girl like her turns up. Bet she never threw up in her life, I thought bitterly. To make matters worse, Jamie was looking at her with that stupid, gobsmacked expression boys have when they see a good-looker. So immature.

'This is Carla,' said the hunk. 'And I'm Pedro.'

The girl smiled again, flashing her eyes over the three of us.

'Maeve, Leo and Jamie,' said Jamie, pointing to each of us in turn without taking his eyes off her.

'We're on a cycling tour,' the girl said. 'Around West Cork.'

'We know,' said Leo. 'Pedro told us. Where are you staying?' Moments ago I'd have been grateful for this kind of questioning, but I'd kind of lost interest since this female appeared.

'In a hostel outside the village,' answered Pedro. 'We tour around from there. It means we don't have to haul all our packs around with us.'

'Your English is very good,' said Jamie. 'You hardly have an accent at all.'

Pedro flashed a toothpaste grin. 'Our mother is English. In spite of living in Spain for the past twenty years, she's still not completely comfortable with the language. She has always only spoken English with us.'

Our mother! Had my ears picked up the right message? Run that by me again.

'Are you brother and sister?' I asked.

They both nodded and I brightened up significantly. The fairy-lights in my brain were flashing again. It was about time I nudged my way into the conversation.

'I like Spanish culture,' I said. 'Don Quixote and the windmills.' (I even got the pronunciation right – *Key-hote-ay*.) Our English teacher had read us bits of the book which is about an old geezer who rides around Spain rescuing people who don't want to be rescued and fighting windmills which he mistakes for giants. It's one of those classy books that Dad says people pretend to have read. Just like I was doing now. 'Great literature that. And the dancing,' I added before they could test me on it. 'I saw some terrific flamingo dancers in the Gaiety

Theatre in Dublin two years ago.'

They looked at me with interest. *That's caught their attention*, I thought. Nothing like a bit of culture to raise people's respect. Then Leo began to laugh and Jamie was smiling. They were all smiling.

'Are you sure it wasn't in the zoo?' spluttered Leo.

'What are you talking about, you daft ignoramus?' I scowled at him.

'Flamingo dancers!' he shrieked, dribbling his coke.

'So?'

Jamie leaned closer to me. 'I think you mean *flamenco* dancers, Maeve,' he whispered.

Oh cripes, what must they think? 'Yeah,' I muttered. 'That's what I said. Flamenco dancers. Why don't you listen?'

Leo wiped his chin with the back of his hand and was about to make some further remark, but Jamie cut in.

'Where are you off to next?' he asked the two Spaniards.

They glanced at one another and hesitated for a moment before Pedro answered.

'We ... we haven't really decided,' he said hastily.

'Well, would you like to come sailing with us tomorrow?' added Jamie enthusiastically. 'My dad's taking us for a sail.'

My blood froze cold. This was the moment I'd been dreading. Okay, I must admit it, as a traveller I'm a bit on the delicate side. The thought of the up and down motion in a yacht, however posh, was enough to activate a hostile reaction in my stomach. I'd already made a show of myself. Did I have to give an encore? I'd have to fast between now and then to make sure there was nothing to throw up. Or I could say I'd a headache – no, too naff. How would I get out of this? I'd be awake all night just thinking about it.

'Oh yes!' 'No thank you,' they both responded together.

Carla was smiling and shaking her head. 'Not me,' she said. 'The sea and I are not friends. I prefer the ground under my feet.'

I looked at her with respect. Now why couldn't I be up front like that? The boys had already accepted her refusal as no big deal. End of story.

'What about you, Pedro?' Jamie switched his attention to her brother. 'Would you like...?'

'Oh yes!' said Pedro again. 'I love to sail.'

'Great!' said Leo. 'This is going to be just mad!'

'I'll stay on land with Carla,' I put in. 'I'll keep her company.'

'No, no,' said Carla. 'There is no need. I don't mind, really I don't. You go with the boys, Maeve. I wouldn't dream of letting you stay back on my account.'

But I shook my head. 'I insist,' I said. 'I can go sailing any old time. I'd be happy to stay with you.'

'Well, if you're sure,' said Carla.

'Absolutely.' I smiled again. Major coup. Not alone had I got out of the nightmare ordeal, but I was seen as an angel of mercy in the process. I looked really meaning-fully at Leo, sensing he was about to make some comment. He clamped his mouth shut – he wanted to be alive and healthy for his precious sail.

We all walked back up the hill together, leaving Carla and Pedro at the lane leading to their hostel.

Carla walked beside me. I was glad to note that she was shorter than me, even though it turned out that, at eighteen, she was four years older. But then, my long, elegant neck gave me that bit of extra height. We stayed chatting for ages – we all got along tremendously well. Funny how you can just click with some people, even after a short time.

'Until tomorrow then,' said Jamie as the late summer chill began to creep up on us.

'At what time?' asked Pedro.

'About nine o'clock,' replied Jamie. He had already shown Pedro the way to the house. It's easy to give directions in a small place like Baltimore.

'See you then,' I said to Carla. 'And I really don't mind not going for a sail,' I added for good measure. Just in case they'd forgotten my big 'sacrifice'.

'This has been the best day in my life,' said Leo, dancing in front of us as we turned towards the house. 'Coming here to this smashing place and seeing boats and meeting new friends. And going sailing tomorrow. I'm so excited.'

'Calm down, Leo,' I said with dignity. But yes, he was quite right. Things were looking decidedly rosy.

5

Carla's Story

Carla was wearing shorts, boots and thick socks when she arrived with Pedro next morning. She looked really good. Too good, from the way Jamie was looking at her.

'I thought perhaps you and I could go for a hike while the others are out sailing,' she said to me.

'What a good idea,' enthused Mrs Stephenson. 'Maeve, there are some small rucksacks in the room where we keep the sailing gear. You can pack yourselves a picnic and go for a ramble.'

Not quite what I'd had in mind. I'd been thinking more of hanging about the harbour to watch the incoming dudes. However, I rose to the occasion.

'Sure,' I said. 'A hike would be great.'

The boys appeared in orange life-jackets which made them look fat and neckless. Except for Pedro. He'd look good in bin-liners.

'Sure you two girls don't want to tag along?' asked Mr Stephenson.

Carla and I both shook our heads.

'They'll have their own fun,' smiled Mrs Stephenson. 'Won't you, girls? Just lock up and put the key under the back door. We'll be back around two o'clock.'

We watched them head down to the dinghy with relief. Then we made up some salad sandwiches and set off on our hike. Carla had been here a few days so she knew the terrain. We went back through the village and beyond it to a hilly road.

'This is the beacon road,' said Carla. 'But we need not

36

keep to it. Let's go the grassy way.'

We clambered over a crumbling stone wall into a rough, hilly field. Carla led the way down into a deep ravine. Facing us across the water was a sheer cliff. Gulls were wheeling around it, making a terrible racket.

'Isn't this nice?' said Carla.

I shivered. The sun couldn't quite make it into this place between the hills. 'Nice?' I said. 'It's like a set for some creepy film.'

Carla laughed. 'I like you, Maeve. You're honest. Come on,' she went on, leading up the hill.

We continued climbing until we came to a huge white beacon at the top of the hill. Below us were rocks against which the sea dashed, sending up sprays of white foam. Across the water we could see the island Jamie had pointed out to us from the house – Sherkin Island. From here it seemed to be only minutes away.

'The ferry is in,' remarked Carla.

Sure enough, a boat was unloading its cargo of people on to some steps. Most of them seemed to be carrying beach gear. Their voices were carried faintly across the expanse of water. I looked around for Carla. She was over at the beacon, looking down at a big yacht that was sailing out of the bay.

'Isn't that the fancy yacht that's been moored farther out?' I asked.

Carla smiled and looked sort of longingly at it. Maybe she was wishing she could be on friendlier terms with the sea so that she could ride in a great galleon of a thing like that. 'Seems like it,' she said.

'Let's give them a wave,' I went on. 'It might be Brad Pitt or Keanu Reeves or someone like that.'

Carla laughed and took up my suggestion.

'There's someone waving back!' I exclaimed, as a figure with a red and white striped teeshirt under his life-jacket waved his arms at us.

'So there is,' giggled Carla.

Encouraged by the thought of being seen by a mega-star or pop king, I waved like mad, using both hands.

'Easy, Maeve,' Carla laughed. 'We don't want them to think we're a couple of loonies. Let's be cool.'

I gave one last wave and then blew a kiss in the direction of the yacht. That was a bit over the top, I know, but opportunities like this don't often present themselves. I looked around for Carla. She was standing looking up at the big white beacon.

'That looks like a round tower gone wrong,' I said. 'They must have forgotten how to do the top bit. Maybe the plans blew away in this wind.'

'This is one of the beacons set up to protect the coast from raiders in the seventeenth century,' said Carla. 'Did you know that the Algerians attacked Baltimore?'

I shook my head. 'How come you know so much about the place?' I asked.

'I was here before,' she said. 'Pedro and I were here with our parents two years ago.'

'And you and Pedro liked it so much you decided to come again on your own?'

She nodded and turned her head away. 'Something like that,' she muttered.

We sat on a grassy bank and I took out the sandwiches. 'Blast,' I said. 'They've gone all soggy.'

Carla laughed, tossing her black, curly hair. 'Never mind,' she said. 'The gulls will eat them.'

Sure enough, when word spread among the gulls that two daft humans were tossing their lunch to all and

sundry, it was soon like a scene from that old Hitchcock film, *The Birds*. They soared and swooped, catching the soggy bits in mid air. Even when every morsel had gone, they hovered round us, looking at us with those gimlet eyes.

'I hope they know we're not on the menu,' I said.

Carla laughed again. 'Don't worry, Maeve. They will get bored and go back to diving for fish.'

It was nice sitting there in the sun. Now and then we heard the phut-phut of a passing motorboat, just enough of an intrusion to remind us that we were not a million miles from civilisation.

'I can see why you wanted to come back,' I said. 'It's pretty nice here in West Cork.'

Carla hesitated for a while before responding.

'Well, there is another reason why we wanted to come back,' she said eventually.

'Yes?' I prompted.

She sat up, hugging her brown knees and gazing at the horizon.

'We're on a sort of a mission, Pedro and I.'

'A mission? Preaching stuff? Do you mean like those bald guys in orange frocks who beat funny drums? Hairy Christians.'

'Hare Krishnas,' Carla laughed, not realising I'd made a great joke. 'No, not that kind of a mission. No, it ... it's something that goes way back to the sixteen hundreds.' She turned to look at me. 'Have you heard of the Battle of Kinsale?' she asked.

'Sure,' I replied.

I'd heard of it all right, but I was a bit short on details. I hoped she wasn't going to ask me any questions that would show me up as a zombie historian – I get glazed eyes and suffer acute deafness during history class.

'Well,' she went on, gazing out to sea again. 'A few Spanish ships left the main flotilla that was heading to Kinsale and they sailed into Castlehaven. They intended to help the O'Driscolls to fight off the English. My ancestor, Don Pedro de Pereda, was in command of one of those ships. But they were attacked by the English.

'Don Pedro escaped, but he knew that the English would be looking for him. The O'Driscolls sheltered him, but he also knew it was only a matter of time before someone would betray him – a dark Spaniard would stand out pretty much against the fair-skinned Irish.'

She put her brown arm alongside mine and laughed. 'See what I mean?'

'Go on,' I said, not wishing to dwell on her golden complexion compared to my freckled one 'What happened to him?'

Carla sighed deeply and looked out to sea. 'We don't

quite know. He never did get back to Spain. But what we *do* know is that, as a reward for trying to help them, the head of the O'Driscoll clan gave him a precious gift which he hid somewhere here in West Cork.'

'Why hide it?' I asked.

'Well, like I said, he never knew when he might be captured. It was the only thing he could do to ensure its safety.'

'Hold on a sec,' I put in. 'How come you know about this gift if your man never got back to Spain? Who told you all this?'

'Oh, the story has been in the family for generations,' said Carla. 'What happened was this: while he was still in hiding, Don Pedro managed to smuggle a message through a trusted friend of the Spanish who was sailing out of Cork on a merchant ship.'

'A message?' I asked. 'Why didn't he send the gift itself?'

Carla was shaking her head. 'That would have been too risky. Ships were always in danger of being attacked by the English, or by pirates, or being sunk in a storm. So it was safer to send a message to his family.'

'And where did he hide the gift?'

'Ha! There's the great question,' laughed Carla. 'All we know is that he hid it somewhere here in West Cork.'

'Brilliant,' I scoffed. 'So all you have to do is dig up all of West Cork to find it. That's easy, Carla. Couple of hundred years and you'll surely find it. Wow, what a great plan your old ancestor came up with.'

With that sort of thinking, it was no wonder lots of Spanish ships ended upside down on rocks. Not that I said this, of course. Sensitive poets don't set out to hurt people's feelings. Could you imagine my fellow-rhymer,

Mister Shakespeare, telling Queen Elizabeth the First that she was a white-faced old gorgon with wispy hair? But I digress.

Carla laughed again. 'Let me finish,' she said. 'The message gave directions to the whereabouts of the gift.'

'But that was as bad as sending the gift itself,' I exclaimed. Was there no end to this imbecility? 'That's like going away from your house and leaving a note stuck to the door saying that the key is under the mat.'

'He wasn't that foolish,' said Carla, almost tartly. 'He wrote the directions very cryptically. Any common thief would not have been able to work them out. He wrote them in the form of a letter. If it had survived, his family would have been able to work out the directions.'

'It didn't survive?'

She shook her head. 'The ship *was* attacked off the Bay of Biscay and, though it didn't sink, it was badly damaged. The message eventually got through to Don Pedro's family, but it was in tatters. Only some of the words are legible.'

'*Are* legible?' I said. 'You mean you've seen this torn letter that dates from the sixteen hundreds?'

'Seen it?' said Carla. 'We have it back at the hostel. This is why Pedro and I came over to Ireland again. Ever since we were told the legend of Don Pedro and this gift, we've been trying to piece it together. Our parents think we're crazy but...well...' she trailed off into a momentary silence. Then she turned and looked at me. 'Desperate problems need desperate remedies.'

'What do you mean?' I asked.

She picked a blade of grass and rolled it between her fingers, as if thinking of a reply.

'My parents,' she began, 'have a vineyard. A small

vineyard, but it has given the family a good living since the seventeen hundreds. Until now.'

'Why?' I asked. 'What's happened?'

Carla sighed and threw down the bit of grass. The wind picked it up and swept it out to sea.

'What's happening,' she went on, 'is that a big multi-national supermarket group, with branches all over Europe, are buying up the smaller vineyards, bottling the wine with their own label and selling it cheaply in their own stores. Most of the vineyards around our area have already sold out and the few that are left can't compete with the lower prices.'

'So they're going to sell out too,' I said.

Carla nodded. 'Except my father. He refuses to sell the vineyard which is part of his heritage. He has already told the Men in Suits what he thinks of them and their big, impersonal, faceless supermarket chain.'

'And is there nothing he can do?' I asked. 'Can he not stop them taking over like that?'

Carla snorted. 'Fat chance,' she said. 'They wave their money and get what they want.'

'Shame,' I said. I know little about wine, except that I put the taste somewhere between paint-stripper and wart lotion, but I got the gist of what Carla was saying. 'But what has all this to do with what we were talking about – this gift?'

She got up and stretched herself.

'Come on,' she said. 'Let's make our way back. They'll soon be back from their sail.'

We made our way back down the steep hill, this time taking the road.

'The gift?' I prompted.

'Promise you won't laugh, Maeve.' She stopped and looked earnestly at me. I crossed my heart and went all intense and serious. This was heavy stuff. 'Well,' she continued, 'if Pedro and I could only crack the whereabouts of that, then my father could use the money to buy up our neighbours' vineyards. Then he could increase his own output and compete with the supermarket chain.'

'Cool,' I said. 'So, what is this gift? Do you know?'

Carla shrugged. 'We're pretty certain it must be gold,' she said. 'That's what the Spanish captains would have been paid for their assistance.'

'Even though the whole thing fell through?' I had to ask. Catch me being fool enough to part with the readies for something that failed miserably.

'I know,' smiled Carla. 'But they did come and they did try. And I know that treasure is out there somewhere. It's only a chance in...in a trillion. But we can't just sit by and watch our father lose everything. Can you understand that?'

I nodded. I couldn't see myself digging up an onion patch, let alone West Cork, for my old man, but I suppose when the chips are down you'll do the weirdest things.

'So, you see, that's what Pedro and I are doing here. Do you think we're stark, raving mad?' She gave a nervous laugh.

'Absolutely bonkers,' I said. 'But I think what you're doing is just great.'

'You do?' She looked relieved. 'Thanks, Maeve. I'm glad you said that. You're a friend.'

'Why don't we tell Jamie and Leo?' I went on, stirred by her praise. 'Who knows, maybe between the lot of us we might come up with a few ideas.'

6

The Ancient Letter

When we got back to the house, the others were just arriving back from their trip in the yacht. They were rosy-cheeked and windblown. I was glad I hadn't gone with them. Apart from everything else, it would have been my nose that got rosy; not a pretty sight.

'Maeve, it was brilliant!' shouted Leo, his eyes glowing with excitement. 'I've learnt loads about sailing. Do you know what a spinnaker is?'

'No,' I laughed. As if I cared.

'It's a special sail that catches a whole load of wind and makes the boat ... yacht go real fast,' went on Leo, unfastening his life-jacket. 'Mr Stephenson put it up to show me how fast the yacht can go. Boy, you should have seen us move!'

Mr Stephenson laughed and put his hand on Leo's shoulder. 'You'll make a first-rate sailor, Leo,' he said. 'You took to it like a duck to water.' He laughed again. 'Although that's not quite the description one should use for a sailor.'

'He was great,' added Mrs Stephenson. 'Very quick to learn, for a boy who's never sailed.'

I didn't know why they were telling me this – as if I was some proud mammy figure revelling in her off-spring's glory.

'Where are Jamie and Pedro?' I asked, just to get the values back on the right footing.

'Tying up the dinghy,' replied Mrs Stephenson. 'Oh, here they are. Pedro, I hope you enjoyed your trip. I expect you do a lot of sailing at home.' She was looking bug-eyed at the handsome Pedro.

'Not as much as I'd like to, Mrs Stephenson,' he said. 'My studies take up a lot of time. Between that and helping my father with the vineyard, my time is rather full.'

'Pedro is studying to be a doctor,' Mrs Stephenson enthused to Jamie. 'You should ask him about the course...'

'Mum, I have no intention of becoming a doctor,' said Jamie, a tad snappily I thought. 'Besides, Pedro is here on holidays. He doesn't want to be talking about studies.'

Mrs Stephenson switched her attention to Carla. 'What about you, dear,' she said. 'What are your plans for the future?'

Carla smiled politely. 'I'll probably follow my mother's footsteps and become a lawyer,' she said.

Mrs Stephenson nodded approvingly. I waited for her to ask me what I intended doing with my life, but either she thought I was too young or else she didn't want to know that I intended becoming a rock star and poet. I'd have held back the Nobel Prize bit – good poets don't brag.

'I'm going to be a film director like Neil Jordan,' volunteered Leo. That was a new one. The week before it was a fish vet or something equally boring.

Mrs Stephenson smiled. 'Yes, dear,' she said. 'Jamie, look after your friends,' she continued. 'Your dad and I are going to Skibbereen to pick up some groceries.'

Pedro looked straight at me and grinned. Wow! Major blush. *Stay cool, Maeve,* I told myself. I undid my rucksack and, just my luck, caught the clasp in the loose-rib stitches of my cotton jumper. Cool is a word not yet

entered into the hard disc of my mind. Of course I got
flustered and ruined the moment as I struggled to free
myself. The more I struggled, the more stitches I un-
ravelled.

'Easy,' laughed Jamie. Ever the classy dude, he lifted
the rucksack and freed the clasp. 'You should have come
with us, Maeve,' he said. 'It was fun. You'd have loved
it.'

'Maybe some other time,' I mumbled. Like when a
world drought would shrivel the oceans.

'And you too, Carla,' said Jamie, turning towards the
diminutive Spaniard as she helped her brother take off his
life-jacket.

'No thanks,' laughed Carla. 'Definitely not.'

'Even though you come from an old sailing background?' I asked, just to show Jamie that I knew more
about Carla than he did.

A puzzled look crossed Pedro's face and he looked
questioningly at his sister. Carla blushed and, to my
delight, looked just as flustered as I had when I'd almost
strangled myself on the rucksack clasp. It's nice to know
you're not alone with your inadequacies.

'I told Maeve about Don Pedro,' she muttered quickly.

But Jamie and Leo picked her up on that remark.

'Who's Don Pedro?' asked Jamie. 'Sounds like someone
from an opera.'

'Or a Mexican bandit,' added Leo. 'Big funny hat and
greasy moustache.'

'Oh, nobody,' said Pedro. 'Just a story. It's nothing.'

Just the sort of remark to make people *thoroughly* interested.

'Go on, tell us,' persisted Leo, jumping to the bait. 'I
love stories. Is he the person you're called after? Are you

a Don yourself? Go on, Pedro, tell us.'

Pedro gave a sickly grin and shot a sharp glance at Carla. He wasn't pleased. He very obviously didn't want to talk about it. Well, that was understandable; it *was* a pretty hairy story.

We went back down to the little shingle beach and sat on some rocks. Pedro looked at Carla again.

'I don't know,' he began doubtfully. 'I feel foolish before I've even said anything.'

'It's all right,' Carla encouraged him. 'Maeve says they'll help us if they can.'

So Pedro told the boys all that Carla had told me. Now and then Carla would interrupt and Jamie would look at her with interest. That bugged me a bit. I know I'd said that Jamie was part brotherly, but I also wanted to keep the other part for myself. But then, I reasoned, Carla is four years older than him. I had the advantage of youth.

THE OLDER WOMAN

By Maeve Morris

She charmed him with her gipsy eyes,
Big and brown like chocolate pies.
'Young lad,' she said, 'we'll go to Spain,
And never come back here again.'
'I can't,' he sighed. 'I love another,
Besides, you're old, so I won't bother.'

'And you have this ancient letter?' Jamie was saying.

'Part of it,' replied Pedro. 'It's badly torn.'

'Can we see it?' asked Jamie. You could sense his brainy mind going click-click.

'It's back at the hostel,' put in Carla. 'Would you like

to see it now?'

Jamie and Leo were on their feet straight away. 'Sure thing,' said Leo. 'Come on. I'm dying to have a look. I've never seen anything that old, except in a museum. I like old things.'

Typical of the child. I glanced at Jamie and then at Carla. I hope Jamie doesn't get to like some old things, I thought. Old things with eyes like pools of oil and hair as black as fresh tar.

We went up a leafy lane to the hostel where Carla and Pedro were staying. There were lots of student types lolling around at wooden tables outside and I'd have liked to hang out there for a while, but you can get too much of a good thing. I stretched my elegant neck and followed the others inside. Carla and Pedro had a small chalet-type room to themselves. I was amazed at how tidy it was. Their sleeping-bags were rolled up at the ends of their bunk beds, their clothes neatly folded on chairs and their very clean towels were hanging out of the window to dry. Not at all like my room. I like to think of my room as artistically Bohemian in keeping with my poetic muse, but Mam said it's a tip.

'Remember to keep your room tidy when you go to Baltimore,' she'd warned me when she was helping me to pack. 'Don't have Jamie's people thinking there's truth in the expression "the dirty Irish".'

'A place should look lived-in,' I'd retorted. 'Makes it comfy.'

'Lived in!' Mam had laughed. 'Died in, more like.'

Pedro drew out a package from his rucksack. Inside was a sort of leather pouch, badly torn. We drew closer and held our breath as he slid out a piece of yellow parchment.

'Wow!' whistled Leo.

Pedro put it on the small table and smoothed it out gently. Like the pouch, it was torn. But you could make out words that were written in some kind of brownish ink.

'It's in Spanish!' I exclaimed, smartly recognising the *els* and *las* and curly thingies on top of some of the letters.

'Of course it's in Spanish,' said Leo. 'Don Pedro was Spanish, you twit.'

'What does it say, Pedro?' asked Jamie.

Pedro pointed out the fragmented words. 'The top bit is fairly legible. It says,' and he began to translate: '"On this day of our Lord 16 ... I write to tell you, my family, that I live and I am in good health, having survived the ravages of ... In my possession I have a valuable ... Fearing for my safety, I have secreted that precious ... in a place known only to me and...In the event of my ... you must seek the cast ... scoll. The legend ... Labh ... a Cluais. Seek the stone that bears the emblem ... arp of barber ... waters that gush...'

He stopped. 'That's all,' he said.

'That's all?' Jamie looked at Pedro incredulously. 'That's all you have to go on?'

Pedro nodded. 'I know. I've said to Carla many times that we haven't a hope of finding this package. But...'

'But I know it's out there somewhere,' burst out Carla. 'I feel it. It's there.'

'The letter is pretty cut up,' said Jamie. 'I wouldn't hold out much hope, Carla.'

But Carla was adamant. 'It's got to be found,' she said with the passion of someone who was convinced that her hopes were founded on fact.

'You're a nutter, Carla,' laughed Leo.

That was enough to spark a response in me. Sisterhood and all that. 'Well, can't we just try,' I said. 'We could be lucky.'

'You'd need more than luck, Maeve,' said Jamie. 'But, hell, we have the time. Let's go for it.'

Everyone brightened up. Me because it would mean more time to bask in Pedro's light; the others for more practical reasons (if you could call looking for some old stuff from the year dot practical). We crowded around the tatty old parchment again.

'Get some paper,' said Jamie. 'You can translate the words that we have and we'll try to work something out.'

We pored over the translation. Every now and then someone would throw out a suggestion which the rest would chew on and dismiss. I yawned. Don Pedro and his crummy treasure were beginning to do my head in.

'Cast,' Jamie was saying. 'Couldn't that mean "*castle*"?'

'Yes,' enthused Pedro. 'We think so. But what is this "scoll"?'

'Is there any word in Spanish that begins or ends in scoll?' asked Jamie.

Carla looked at Pedro and they both shook their heads.

'Schull!' exclaimed Leo. 'That could be Schull. It's only a few miles from here. Will we go and dig up around Schull?'

'Get real, Leo,' I said. 'Different spelling. "Scoll" has nothing to do with skull. Besides there must be millions of skulls...'

'No,' put in Jamie. 'Leo means Schull. It's a village near here.' He turned back to the letter. 'Cast,' he mused again. 'We could at least be pretty sure of that one, wouldn't you think?'

Pedro was nodding. ' Probably is. But,' he looked doubtful, 'there are dozens of castles in West Cork. Dozens.'

'I know,' sighed Jamie. 'But it's a start. Come on and we'll have a look at the one in the village. I don't expect anything, but this whole thing is a lottery anyway. We could just be lucky. No harm to have a look around.'

Carla's face lit up. 'See, Pedro?' she said. 'Now we have help. Already we have somewhere to start.'

Pedro nodded. 'Don't get your hopes up too high, sis. We're still a long way from ...'

'I know, I know,' said Carla. 'But at least we must try.'

'Bring the translation with you,' suggested Jamie. 'We might get some ideas while we're having a look around.'

Leo was hopping up and down like a demented flea. 'Deadly,' he said. 'This is just deadly.'

7

Caught Trespassing

There were very worn steps leading up to the castle which looked out over the small harbour. Inside, the place was rather disappointing. You'd expect a castle to have some sort of historic vibes floating about. You know, vibes of dashing heroes swashing and buckling their way through high chambers. But no. Major disappointment. All that was left inside the stone walls were old Coke cans and a few plastic bags. We looked around, no one wanting to be the one to say that this was a waste of time.

'Where should we begin?' asked Pedro, eventually. 'We don't even know what we're looking for.'

Leo, bless his nerdish little heart, was pulling ivy from one of the walls. We watched him for a while before we all set to, doing the same thing and kidding ourselves into feeling we just might be doing something useful. Which, of course, we weren't. We talked about Don Pedro and his gift and came up with offbeat suggestions as to what he might have done with it. Now and then Jamie would stop and look at the bit of paper that he'd written the translation on.

'He definitely hid it,' he said.

'We know that, cleverclogs,' I put in. 'That's why we're searching for the silly thing.'

'What are you kids doing here?'

We jumped as a deep voice rasped at us from the doorway. We turned to see a thick-set man with mousey hair and a porridge complexion scowling at us. How long had he been standing there listening to us? How much had he heard? We looked at him rather foolishly.

'What are you at?' he asked again. His accent was pure Cork.

Pedro cleared his throat. 'We're not doing any harm,' he said. 'We...we're just clearing some of the ivy so that we can see these historic walls.'

The man's lip curled when he picked up on Pedro's slight accent. Then Jamie put his spoke in.

'It's a shame to let an historic place like this just crumble away,' he said. 'We thought we'd do a bit of clearing.'

His English accent seemed to spark off the man's anger. 'You foreigners,' he exploded. 'You think you can come here and tell us what to do with our ruins. Mind your own business. If you pull that ivy off, the walls really will crumble. It's the ivy is holding the stones together. Now get out of here or I'll call the guards.'

Carla looked scared and the boys looked flustered and embarrassed. Time for Maeve to save the situation.

'Keep your shirt on, sunshine,' I said sweetly. 'We haven't come here to do damage. We ... we're doing a bit of historical research. This man,' I nodded towards Pedro, he being the oldest of us, 'is an archaeologist. A Spanish archaeologist,' I added for extra emphasis. 'He's researching old castles.' I could see Jamie roll his eyes to heaven. What had I done now?

'Yeah,' retorted the man. 'And I'm the king of Ireland. Now get out of here, the lot of you.'

'Nutter,' I mumbled as we slunk out. 'Himself and his pathetic pile of rocks.'

Jamie grinned and put his hand on my shoulder. 'Cool it, Maeve,' he said. 'He's obviously being protective of his heritage and doesn't want a bunch of strangers sniffing around. How was he to know we're perfect angels?'

'Your trouble, Jamie,' I said, 'is that you keep seeing the good in people. Why can't you be like me and ...'

'And cast them into outer darkness before they've had a chance to prove themselves,' he finished.

'Something like that,' I replied.

Jamie laughed and shook his head. 'You're crooked as ever, Maeve Morris,' he said.

We went across the road and sat at one of the tables overlooking the harbour.

'This is hopeless,' said Pedro. 'We're only going to make fools of ourselves. What do you say we forget this whole thing and just concentrate on a holiday?'

I nodded. That was fine by me. Traipsing around West Cork with a tatty letter and scraping ivy off stupid ruins was not up to much. Certainly not. But Carla was almost in tears.

'But poor Papa,' she said. 'He will lose everything. In two months everything will change...'

'What do you mean?' asked Jamie.

'What she means,' said Pedro, 'is that our father has only two months to come up with the money to buy out our two neighbours. They are on his side – they want to sell to him rather than to the supermarket chain. But they've been hit even worse than us by the competition. Their backs are to the wall. They've told Father that they'll last for another two months. If he doesn't come up with the money by then, they'll have no choice but to sell to the big boys.' He turned to Carla and put his arm around her shoulders. 'I know it's hopeless, sis,' he said. 'But what more can we do?'

Carla bit her lip. A tear trickled down her cheek. Leo looked at me and raised his eyebrows questioningly. Well, I didn't know what to say either. Big business and grape farms were way out of my league.

But Jamie wasn't about to let the moment pass. I'd often chortled at some movie or other where a woman would suddenly turn on the tears and everyone would fall about trying to please her. Here was living proof that the ploy works. Jamie leaned over and all but patted her hand.

She's old, I consoled myself. *It won't last.*

'We'll have another go,' he said. He looked at Pedro. 'One more try at working something out, okay?'

Pedro looked doubtful, but he nodded. Now Leo was in on the act. By golly, what a drop of water from the eyes can do!

'We'll search everywhere, Carla. We'll find Don Pedro's treasure.'

'God, you make it sound like some cruddy fairy story,' I said. 'Get real. Can't you see how impos...' I broke off as the word 'unpopular' loomed large in my mind. I'd better not be the one to shoot the project because I'd be shooting myself in the foot. When I'd removed it from my mouth, that is.

'Look, let's forget about it for the moment,' said Pedro in a grown-up authoritative way. 'Who'd like a Coke?'

We sat over our drinks and tried to jolly along the rest of the afternoon. The bustle and noise in the small harbour cheered us up. The big yacht was back, still moored away out. They hadn't gone very far on their trip. We tried to imagine the sort of people who owned it.

'U2,' I said.

Both Carla and Pedro looked startled.

'What?' said Pedro.

'U2,' I said again. 'You must have heard of U2, the pop group?'

Pedro smiled. 'Oh yes,' he said. 'U2.'

Traffic frequently got jammed on the narrow street, but no one seemed to mind. Even when the driver of a bread van double parked outside the supermarket down the road, drivers waited patiently until he'd delivered his goods. The name O'Driscoll was written in big red letters across the back doors of the van. The wind blew one of the doors open, splitting the name in two.

Leo interrupted my observation of the passing scene.

'Hey,' he said, pointing to a notice outside McCarthy's pub at the corner of the paved area where we were sitting. 'There's a group playing there tonight.'

'So?' I said.

'Could we go?' he asked eagerly. 'It'd be great.'

'Leo, my dear tiny cousin,' I laughed. 'Whatever hope the rest of us have of getting into a pub, you haven't a hope in hell.'

'No, it will be all right,' said Pedro. 'I've seen whole families in there at night listening to the music. It's a very friendly place.'

Leo gave me a triumphant look, but I was too pleased at the prospect of spending an evening in Pedro's company to respond.

We were decidedly chirpy as we left Carla and Pedro at the lane leading to their hostel.

'Until eight o'clock then,' said Pedro.

'Looking forward to it,' I said, sophisticated as you like.

I was still smiling as we went the rest of the way. Leo looked at me and gave a sly grin. 'Maeve's in love,' he sang.

'Give over,' I muttered, but I was pleased to see Jamie look my way.

'You got your hair cut,' he said. Lord, was it only now he was beginning to notice *me?* And why did it have to be the hair that he noticed? I'd almost forgotten the cruddy haircut. 'It's nice,' he went on. 'I like it.'

'You do?'

He nodded.

'If you like lavatory brushes,' put in Leo.

'Don't be silly, Leo,' said Jamie, still looking at me. 'It looks trendy.'

Well, a bit of intrigue, a dashing Spaniard, praise from Jamie, a night's fun in the offing – this had been some day. There wasn't much else one could ask from life.

8

My Brilliant Deduction

Jamie's mother was drying her blonde hair when we arrived back. She'd been swimming off the shingle beach. 'Salad's ready,' she said. 'Set it up there, Jamie, and we'll eat. Your friends must be starving.'

The way she said it, as if Leo and I were a couple of urchins who'd followed Jamie home, gave me a moment of teeth-gritting. But I'd promised my mother that I'd stick to a code of politeness, so I simply smiled.

'Yes,' I said. 'We're all hungry. And thanks for having us here, Mrs Stephenson.' I squeezed the words out painfully. Grovelling doesn't come naturally to me.

She paused from her hair-drying and looked at her son. Jamie had tensed slightly. 'You're welcome, dear,' she said, still looking at Jamie. For some reason the image of my own cosy mum came to mind and, for one brief, intense moment, I missed her. But only for a moment. We pulled out the old-fashioned-but-trendy pine chairs and sat around the table.

'Wash your hands, Leo,' I said, feeling it was time to show that we no longer swung from trees and grunted, whatever Mrs Cordelia Lyn Stephenson might think.

He looked at me in amazement. 'Huh?' he said. I might have known my subtle attempt at civilised procedures would go right over his head.

'Your hands,' I hissed as good-naturedly as I could. 'Wash them before your meal.'

'Wash your own paws,' he retorted. 'I've already washed. I always do,' he added, just to add to my discomfort.

'Stop bossing me, anyway.'

I could see Jamie tensing up again. He thought we were going to let him down by more bickering, so I just grinned idiotically and swallowed hard. This was becoming one prickly scene. Well, at least there was no special invalid food for me this time. Hopefully they'd all forgotten my throwing-up incident. I watched the time intently as we ate. How would I word this? How would I say it without appearing impolite? How would I cut across the conversation. I took a deep breath.

'Excuse me,' I said, 'I wonder would you mind if I watched *Home and Away*?'

Mrs Stephenson looked up at me, a spoonful of raspberry mousse poised half-way to her face.

'Home and away?' she queried.

'Australian soap,' muttered Jamie, with what I thought was a tad on the disapproval side. His mother laughed. 'Oh dear me, no,' she said. 'No telly here, Maeve.'

No telly? What sort of freaks were these people?

Mr Stephenson leaned towards me. 'That's one of the conditions of a holiday home, Maeve,' he explained. 'No telly and no phones. Most people who own holiday homes are busy types, always at the end of a telephone or fax machine. Always aware of news and current affairs. While we're here, we just want to switch off the world and relax. See?'

I saw. *There always has to be a downside*, I thought.

'We read,' said Jamie, still in that disapproving way. 'We relax by reading.'

Leo snorted into his dessert. 'Should have brought your Noddy books, Maeve.'

'It's all right,' I said with what I thought was superb control and dignity. 'I'll ring Mam and ask her to record ite.' See if I was going to give in to highbrow pressure.

'Speaking of books,' Jamie turned to his father. Oh no, I thought. Here we go – *who's read what by whom and wasn't it just the most wonderful novel and isn't he/she just the greatest writer and what have you read recently, Maeve?* 'Are there any books here that would give a history of West Cork?' he asked.

At first I cringed, but then I realised what he was after.

His dad indicated the shelves of books on the far side of the room.'I expect you'll find what you want over there,' he said. 'I haven't checked out the reading matter, but knowing the Jacksons I'd say they have books of local interest. There's certainly one on the old Cork families – the O'Driscolls and MacCarthys and so on. Why?'

Jamie looked slightly sheepish. 'Just wondered,' he said. 'We might explore a bit and it would be nice to know the background.'

'Splendid idea,' said Mr Stephenson. He looked across at his wife with one of those meaningful glances peculiar to adults. 'By the way,' he went on, 'we were thinking of taking a trip around to Glengarriff. Just an overnight. Back tomorrow evening. You're all welcome to come...'

For one stomach-lurching moment I thought Jamie was going to say yes. Leo's eyes lit up – there was no doubt which choice he'd make. But Jamie was shaking his head. 'No, we'll stay put. We've sort of said we'd tour around with Pedro and Carla.'

'Nice couple, Pedro and Carla,' put in Mrs Stephenson. 'He was telling me all about their vineyard.'

'You asked, you mean,' muttered Jamie, his dark eyes glittering harshly. 'Does that make him measure up, Mother? Will that do?'

I watched with amazement this exchange between

Jamie and his mother. This was a totally alien side to his nature which I hadn't seen before. What was going on?

Mrs Stephenson's face registered annoyance. 'Really, Jamie,' she began.

'Jamie!' said Mr Stephenson sharply. 'That's quite enough.'

'Sorry,' mumbled Jamie.

Shoot! Just when I thought I was about to enjoy an upper-class ding-dong, he goes and apologises. Typical of the lad. I tried to use telepathy to urge him into taking a stand, but it didn't work.

We ate in silence for a while. I wasn't comfortable with this atmosphere and was beginning to think I'd have been better off at home hanging out with my bunch of schoolmates.

'About Glengarriff,' said Mr Stephenson eventually.

Leo and I both looked at Jamie. He was shaking his head. 'No,' he said. 'Really, we'd prefer to stay around here. You two go ahead.'

Jamie's parents seemed relieved. They probably hadn't fancied taking two greenhorns on a sail like that. Not to mention the possibility of me throwing up all over their nice clean yacht.

'Don't forget about the bikes, if you're touring around,' said Mrs Stephenson, being helpful now that things had worked out in her favour. 'I'm sure Maeve and Leo would enjoy that, wouldn't you, dear?' She turned to me and turned on that sweet smile – sweet as honey on an unripe lemon. 'You do cycle?'

Cordelia Lyn, I told myself, before I could utter some milk-curdling retort. *Her name is Cordelia Lyn. When she kicks the bucket, that daft name will be engraved on her tombstone.*

'Bikes?' said Leo. I knew what he was thinking – bikes were a major come-down from a yacht. I almost felt sorry for him. Only almost.

'That's right.' Jamie looked pleased. 'There are three or four mountain bikes in the utility room. That means,' he turned to me, 'we can all tour around together.'

I caught his drift. With the bikes, we could travel much greater distances in our search for old man Pedro's stuff. Not that we were going to get anywhere near that, I figured, but we'd all be able to hang out together.

It was while I was up in my room, searching through my bundle of tops for something suitably impressive, that the mind-bending revelation burst upon my conscious-ness. My Oasis tee-shirt was folded in such a way that the word 'sis' was all that was visible. I laughed to myself at the possibility of wearing something with just 'sis' on it. And then I remembered the van door that had been swinging in the wind earlier on outside the supermarket. 'O'Dri' was all that remained on the left-hand side, the 'scoll' was hidden. 'Scoll' ... O'Driscoll!

'So that's what the "scoll" means,' I said aloud. 'Leo, Jamie!' I tore across the landing to the boys' room. They looked up, startled. 'Listen,' I gasped, ignoring Leo's skinny torso as he struggled into a sweater. 'That word "scoll" in the letter. I know what it means!'

Jamie was looking at me as if I had two heads. 'What?'

'It's O'Driscoll!' I went on. 'It's all that's left of the word O'Driscoll. We're looking for O'Driscoll's castle. That's an old Cork name, isn't it? Your dad said so.'

Realisation dawned on Jamie. He slowly smiled.

'Cripes, you could be right. An O'Driscoll castle. *That's* what we're looking for. Well done, Maeve.'

I blushed, especially when I remembered that I had a

load of clips and mousse in my hair to try and flatten it
down. Oh well, now it meant that we could shuffle
around this O'Driscoll castle, find the gold or whatever
and have enough time left over to have a brill holiday.

We met Carla and Pedro on their way up the hill to call
for us. Carla was wearing a white sleeveless top which
showed off her golden complexion sickeningly well. I was
glad I had on a long-sleeved sweatshirt to hide my
freckled stick-arms. However I made up for it by sporting
a pretty choker necklace I'd picked up in an Oxfam shop
for twenty pee. It emphasised my elegant neck.

'We know something new!' Leo shouted to them.
'We're looking for O'Driscoll's castle!'

I bit back my fury at his stealing my brilliance. But I
needn't have worried, Jamie did his gentlemanly bit.
'Maeve came up with the answer,' he said and then went
on to elaborate. I felt really clever.

'Well, that narrows it down a bit,' said Pedro, looking
at me. I felt positively brilliant. Sparks of pure intellect
flew from my eyes.

'A bit,' agreed Jamie. He gave me a sheepish look. 'It's
great that you've worked out that it's an O'Driscoll
castle, Maeve. But there are scads of them scattered
around the county.'

My heart sank. 'Do you mean it's not just one castle?'

Jamie nodded. 'I'm afraid there are lots of O'Driscoll
castles. There were the top dogs around here, so they had
places dotted all around.'

Major let-down. 'You sure?' I asked.

Jamie nodded again. 'I read a guide to West Cork on
my way over with the parents. I always like to know the
territory I'm visiting,' he added, almost apologetically.

'Well, blast!' I uttered. My light had faded somewhat.

However, on the positive side, we still had an evening's jollifications to look forward to.

McCarthys was pretty full, but we managed to squash into a niche near the band. They were pretty good, not in a classy, head-banging way, but okay for a small village at the bottom of Ireland. With the loud music and loud laughter and talk and the hordes of people it was all rather heady.

'This is mad,' beamed Leo.

'Mad mad,' I laughed and shouted back.

MAD MUSIC

By Maeve Morris

She listened to the drummer
And thought he looked so cool,
With torn jeans and tee-shirt
And eyes that made her drool.
But, 'Steady on,' she told herself,
'And don't be such a fool.
Already you have two loved ones
Whose hearts you want to rule.'

Sitting facing the window, I looked at my reflection and tried flattening down my hair. Then I tried the Kate Winslet look. I was startled and embarrassed when I saw two faces looking in at me. One of them I recognised as the geezer who'd run us out of the castle. The other, a man with one of those black woolly hats with a rolled rim, was smiling in at me. I cringed and blushed and switched my attention to Pedro.

After a few minutes the woolly-hatted man elbowed his way through the crowd and was heading our way.

Oh lord, I thought. *He's fallen for me and has come to ask me out. I'll die.* But, thankfully, he went past us and greeted a group at the next table. He mustn't have been looking at me at all, I figured with relief. I'd cringed for nothing.

Later on, when the group had finished their gig, there was still a buzz of talk and laughter as everyone stayed on. The atmosphere was relaxed and happy. And so was Jamie. My earlier fears that he was turning into some prat seemed to be unfounded. This was the Jamie I knew and was comfortable with. Just to make sure of where I stood in his scheme of things, I put my elbows on the table and gave him that wide-eyed look I'd been practising.

'What's wrong with you, Maeve?' asked Leo. 'You look like something undead, all staring popped-out eyes. The Thing from the Swamp.'

I sighed and withdrew my elbows. Pedro looked at me and smiled. 'Little brothers, eh?' he said sympathetically.

'Cousin,' I said emphatically. 'He's only a cousin.'

'Never mind,' said Pedro. 'You're certainly not pop-eyed. You look really good.'

Wow! I glanced at Jamie to make sure he'd heard. He was talking to Carla, the older woman. I looked at Pedro and wondered if I should ask him to say all that again in a louder voice. Then Jamie leaned towards Pedro.

'Let's have another look at that translation,' he said. 'Did you bring it with you?'

Pedro nodded and fished it out of his pocket. I groaned inwardly. Surely we weren't going to waste good chatting time poring over that stupid thing. This was not the moment for Don bally Pedro and his dicey gold. Once more the paper was smoothed out and once more we looked at it.

'Still looks the same,' I said.

'What?' Jamie looked up at me.

'The letter. It's just as puzzling now as it was this afternoon.'

Jamie shrugged. 'If we keep looking at it, we might gradually get to piece it together,' he said.

And pigs might fly, I thought.

'"Having survived the ravages of,"' quoted Jamie. 'I suppose he means the ravages of *war*. "Fearing for my safety I have secreted that precious..." Well, that has to be the treasure,' he went on. '"In the event of my..."'

'That has to be *death*,' Leo got in on the act. '"In the event of my *death*".'

Pedro nodded. 'It's the next bit that is the puzzling part,' he said. '"You must seek the ..."'

'*The O'Driscoll castle*,' Jamie broke in. He was shouting

to make himself heard over the noise. 'That stuff just has
to be in an O'Driscoll castle.'

'All we have to do is find the right one,' snorted Pedro.
He shook his head and turned to Carla. She frowned and
pulled his arm.

'Don't go filling us all with doubts again, Pedro,' she
said. 'We simply *have* to work this out.'

Pedro held up his hands placatingly. 'All right, all
right,' he said. 'But don't be too hopeful, Carla. I don't
want to see you disappointed.'

Touching. A stab of envy pierced my armour; I wondered what it must be like to have an older brother. But
then, I reasoned, if I did have an older brother, he'd
probably be just a bigger, older version of Leo. I dis-
missed the thought.

'"The legend",' went on Jamie, 'I wonder what that
could be. Are there any O'Driscoll legends?'

'What could a legend have to do with the stuff he hid?'
asked Leo in his high-pitched voice. 'A legend is only a
story. Whatever he hid is real, isn't it?'

'Yes, it's real,' said Carla very firmly.

'Why are you so sure it's gold?' asked Jamie. 'It sounds
a bit ... you know ... story-bookish. Buried Spanish gold
and all that.'

'Nothing story-bookish about it,' snapped Carla. 'I
know it's out there.' She glanced at Pedro, who nodded
slightly. 'I don't actually know if it *is* gold,' she admitted.
'But it is something very precious. If we could just piece
together this local legend I know we'd...'

She broke off as the man with the woolly hat turned
around. He was well past his sell-by date, somewhere in
his forties with a weather-beaten tanned face. There were
good-natured laughter lines around his eyes and his sharp

jaw would have looked well on any groovy film dude you'd care to mention. If he'd been a bit younger I'd have craned my elegant neck. His clothes were the sort worn by everyone else around these parts – sea-faring gear.

'Sorry,' he said in a strong Cork accent. 'I couldn't help overhearing. I'm pretty well up on local legends. Was there something particular you wanted to know?'

There was an awkward pause when we realised that our conversation had gone beyond our own circle. There was a bit of shuffling and glancing at one another. The man shrugged and seemed about to turn back to his own companions. It suddenly dawned on me that this Corkman just might be able to help us in our quest. He might know the legend that would put us on the right track. I couldn't let the moment pass.

'Do you know any O'Driscoll legends?' I asked.

He turned towards us again and laughed. 'There are lots of O'Driscoll legends,' he said. 'The O'Driscolls are a very historic family.'

'We know that,' I said, warming to the fact that I was doing my bit to solve our problem and impressing Jamie and Pedro into the bargain. And Carla. 'But do you know anything of a legend about hidden treasure?' I felt rather than heard Jamie's sharp intake of breath. Good, I *was* impressing him with my neat line of questioning.

'Treasure?' the man's eyebrows shot up.

'Yes,' I went on. 'Did you ever hear about a Spaniard who was given something precious by the O'Driscolls back in the...' I looked at Pedro to see if I had the date right, but he had his head in his hands. Probably the heat, I thought. It *was* pretty hot in this crowded place. 'The sixteen hundreds,' I continued. 'A Spaniard who came to help the O'Driscolls against the English. Did you ever hear that story?'

The man was shaking his head. 'New to me,' he said. 'But, listen to me, are you staying around for a while? I could look it up for you if you like.'

I was positively glowing now. Maeve to the rescue. 'You could?' I said, looking at the others in turn. Except for Leo, who was beaming, Pedro, Jamie and Carla were looking a bit miffed. I put it down to jealousy of my quick thinking. I switched my attention back to the helpful Corkman.

'That would be great, wouldn't it?' I gave the others another chance to share my enthusiasm. 'This man will find out the legend for us.'

Pedro was the first to thaw. 'Very good. Thank you,' he nodded.

'Pedro is Spanish,' I said eagerly. 'He's got an ancient letter ... ouch!' I stopped as a foot kicked my ankle. It hadn't been Leo. I glanced at the other three. Jamie was looking at me with pursed lips. Jamie! Now what was that in aid of? He made great play of looking at his watch. 'Look at the time,' he said. 'We really must be going.'

'I'll be here tomorrow, about midday,' the man said. 'If you come then I might be able to lay hands on that story for you. A Spaniard who helped the O'Driscolls, you say?'

I nodded. 'And a precious thingummy,' I said. 'If you could find out anything about a precious gift.'

The others were on their feet now. I smiled at the helpful Corkman to make up for their bad grace and followed them out.

9

A Showdown with Jamie

'What did you want to go telling that man – a stranger - about our business, Maeve?' said Jamie when we got outside. I swallowed hard. This did not fit the picture I'd had about me being the voice of reason and intelligence.

'It's all right,' put in Pedro. But before I could bask in his taking my side he added, 'The damage is done. We'll just have to go along with it.'

I stopped in the middle of the road. 'What's going on?' I asked. 'What's with the long faces and bad vibes?'

'We don't need others knowing what we're at,' said Jamie. 'I know you meant well, Maeve, but...'

'But, me eye!' I exclaimed angrily. 'You heard this geezer, he's going to try and find the legend for us. If I hadn't asked we'd still be in the dark. That cruddy letter is as much use as ... as a dead mackerel as it is. We need any help we can get.' I looked at Carla for approval, but she just looked at me sympathetically.

'It's a private matter,' went on Jamie.

'It's a private matter!' I mimicked his English accent and held my nose, just to be more effective. 'It's so private that it'll lie in a hole in the ground somewhere forever and ever. Wake up, Jamie. Pedro and Carla wouldn't have a hope in hell of finding that gift thing without a bit of help. There's no way anyone could decipher that stupid letter.'

But Jamie was shaking his head. 'We'll manage on our own,' he began. 'We don't want a crowd of treasure seekers out digging up the county.'

'Okay, Mister Brainbox,' I retorted. 'What's the next move, then? Go on, work out the few torn words and give us all a thrill.'

'Please,' Pedro interrupted. 'I have said it does not matter. Let's leave it alone.' He turned to me and focused his large brown eyes on me. 'Maeve,' he said softly, and my knees weakened. 'Just let's leave this project between us. Please don't ask anyone else's advice, okay?'

I wanted to die. Just lie down and die right there in the middle of this crummy road in this crummy village in this crummy county. But not before I'd let these nerds have an earful.

'This whole thing is just stupid,' I said. 'Some stupid old sailor in a tin hat writes a stupid letter about legends and castles and centuries later we all get our knickers in a knot over it. He was probably mouldy drunk when he wrote it. He'd probably drunk a bucket of rum and wrote that load of nonsense while he was seeing pink elephants. West Cork pink elephants, what's worse. I thought we'd come here for a holiday. If you think I'm going to spend my days sniffing around piles of rotten castles you can think again.' My voice had gone several pitches higher by now.

'You're absolutely right,' said Pedro.

I should have been grateful that he was agreeing with me, but my anger was transporting me beyond all reason. I turned on him, eyes blazing.

'Don't patronise me, you...you Spanish person,' I almost spat. 'I'm sorry I came to this godforsaken dive. I'm going back to pack my stuff. I'll be gone tomorrow. Come on, Leo.'

Leo gaped at me. 'Huh?'

'We're leaving,' I said.

'Speak for yourself,' he retorted.

I should have known. That bit about blood being thicker than water is all my eye. I stormed off into the night.

'Maeve, wait!' Jamie ran after me.

'Don't spin me any yarns about wanting me to stay,' I said, my anger in full flow like a regal ship. 'Your old lady doesn't like me and you've become a right prat. Leave me alone.' I raced ahead, heart pounding. God, it was good to get roaring angry now and then. Great for the circulation.

Mr and Mrs Stephenson were in the kitchen area packing food for their trip to Glengarriff. 'Oh, you're all

back,' said Mrs Stephenson. 'Did you have a nice time?'

'No, it's just me,' I said evenly. 'I ... I came on ahead of the others.'

'Are you not feeling well, dear?' Her look of concern made me even madder. Did she think I spent my whole life throwing up? Was there no end to this?

I muttered something and charged up the stairs.

Later that night there was a tap on my door. If it was the Honourable Lady Mrs Cordelia Lyn Nose-in-the-Air Stephenson with tea and toast, I'd go bananas.

It was Jamie. I pretended to be asleep. It's difficult to do that convincingly when sitting bolt upright in a window seat. He came over and sat beside me.

'I know you're awake. I can see your eyes moving,' he said.

'Get lost,' I replied.

'Listen, Maeve,' he went on. 'About what you said...'

'Yeah?'

'About my mother and all that. Well, I just want you to know that it has nothing to do with you. Mum and I are going through a bit of a ...'

'A bit of aggro?' I prompted.

'Yes, I suppose you could call it that. Aggro. You see, she's always managed my life. Apart from boarding-school, she's always made my decisions for me. Organised my friends – who I invited for weekends and holidays and all that.' He was twisting his fingers nervously. Where was all this leading?

'A control freak, is she?' I said. I didn't add that I'd had his ma sussed out long ago.

Jamie nodded. 'I suppose you could say that. I never minded,' he went on.' I'm pretty easy-going, as you know.

Until lately, that is. I suppose I've done a bit of growing up, but I want to make my own decisions now. Do things my own way.'

'Hmmpff. At fourteen it's taken you long enough,' I said. 'Aren't you a bit long in the tooth to be showing a spark of individuality? The rest of us *normal* people do that at the age of four.'

'Yeah, I know. I know. But the result is that Mum looks disapprovingly at anything I take on independently of her.'

'Like asking me and Leo here.'

'Yes,' he grinned. 'More than anything I've wanted you to be here with me. You're fun.'

Was that plural or singular? I wondered. But I didn't ask. He might have said plural. A girl has to hang on to her illusions. 'Your mum didn't like the idea,' I stated.

'Like I said, it's nothing to do with you. She'd like to think that I'm still some little wimp who'll come on holidays with herself and Dad and cause no trouble, just go where they go and do what they do. A bit over-protective, I suppose.'

'Gross,' I said. 'Deadly boring. You must have been a right wimp before you bumped into Leo and me.'

He laughed. 'Well, it's to do with her not being around a lot,' he went on. 'Most of the year I'm at boarding-school. Then, when I do get holidays, both she and Dad are not around much. Dad travels a lot, as you know.'

I nodded. 'Big noise in the UN,' I said. 'But what about your old ... your mum?'

'She's an architect. A pretty good one, ' he added with a touch of pride. So, she could draw houses. Big deal. 'But her work is demanding,' he continued. 'She doesn't get a lot of free time to be with me when I'm at home. So you see, when we get our precious summer holidays together, she gets a bit possessive...'

'And disapproving,' I couldn't help adding.

'No, Maeve. Not at all. She just feels that I should spend all my time with her and Dad. She has nothing against you or Leo. She's just being ...'

'Disapproving,' I said again. 'Don't deny it. I'm not blind. She thinks Leo and me are not up to scratch for her precious son.' I could feel myself getting tetchy again.

'Please, will you shut up and listen. She just would prefer if I didn't have *anyone* to hang around with, that's all.'

Selfish old bat, I thought.

'So, that's why you're all tense when we're all together,' I said 'You think Leo and I are going to let you down?'

He looked a bit nonplussed and hesitated before he answered. 'I suppose I want to show her that I can make good friends,' he said. 'That *my* choices are important.'

'What's that supposed to mean?' I'd never been called a choice before, and I didn't like it.

Jamie's face twisted as he struggled for an answer. But I put in my spoke first. 'So you don't want Leo and me making eejits of ourselves, huh?' I said.

He shuffled a bit.

'Well, don't worry, sunshine.' I let the power run through my veins. 'We won't hang around to let you down. Better get on the phone to Mama's approved pussycats to come and fill the gap, because me and Leo are out of here.'

'Oh, Maeve,' he said in exasperation. 'Could we not begin all over again? I'm sorry you picked up the wrong vibes. Don't go all weird on me. I really want you to stay. It would be no fun without you.'

I savoured the moment. 'Say it again,' I said.

'Say what again?'

'The bit about really wanting me to stay.'

'I do. I really want you to stay. Believe me.'

'Okay then. But no more tetchiness. I am who I am and that's how it has to be. I don't put on any acts for disapproving mums or anyone else, all right? And I'll only torture Leo away from the house.'

Jamie nodded and grinned. I knew then that the air was cleared for a better outlook on this holiday. Anyway, I consoled myself, Mrs Cordelia Lyn Stephenson would be heading for Glenwhatsit tomorrow. With any luck she'd be marooned on some gull-infested rock until my holiday was over.

10
Pete

Mr and Mrs Stephenson had already left when I came down the next morning.

'Hi,' said Jamie as I yawned my way down the open staircase. He was looking very bright and cheerful as he ladled out some cornflakes.

'Folks gone?' I asked. He nodded. 'Good,' I said pointedly. 'Now you can relax.'

Leo looked up at me, milk dribbling down his chin. 'Maeve!' He glanced anxiously at Jamie. 'That's a horrible thing to say.'

'Jamie knows what I mean,' I said.

But Jamie just pursed his lips and said nothing. Oops, foot in mouth again. Cool it, Maeve.

'I mean...' I began.

'Yes, yes. We know what you mean,' muttered Jamie. 'Let's leave it, okay?'

We sat in silence for a few minutes. Nothing could be heard but the chomp chomp of cereal.

'I think we should go to Castletownshend,' Jamie said eventually.

'Castletown what?' I asked, helping myself to more sustenance.

'Castletownshend,' he went on. 'That's the place near where the Spanish flotilla came in. There's an O'Driscoll castle there.'

'But what about that man who said he'd meet us this morning?' I asked. 'He might have some valuable information. It's worth a try,' I added encouragingly. As I

was the one who had instigated this, I was blooming sure
I was going to explore all possibilities. Especially when it
meant letting someone else do the work for us. Jamie
mulled over this as he stirred his tea.

'Well, okay,' he said. 'We'll see what he has to say.
Then we'll head for Castletownshend.'

Carla and Pedro were surprised when we turned up at
the hostel on bikes. I hung back a bit, conscious of my
outburst of last night, what with calling their ancestor a
drunk in a tin hat and all that. But they both treated me
as if nothing had happened.

'The bikes mean we can cycle to loads of O'Driscoll
castles,' enthused Leo.

Great, I thought. Cycle together – yes. Shuffle around
dreary ruins – no. If the Corkman with the woolly hat
had found the right story, then maybe we'd know once
and for all about the so-called treasure and we could get
on with doing more groovy things with our time.

Sure enough, he was sitting at one of the barrels
outside Bushe's. In spite of the hot sun, he still wore the
woolly hat.

'Hi,' I said eagerly as we gathered around him. The
wrinkles around his eyes deepened as he grinned. 'The
treasure hunters,' he said.

I could see Pedro stiffen a bit. As a university student
he'd hardly want to be identified with what seemed like
some sort of kids' story-book plot.

'Were you able to find out anything?' I asked.

'About the legend,' put in Leo. 'You said you could
find out about the legend.'

'Hold on there,' laughed the man, his dark eyebrows
disappearing up under the rolled rim of his hat. 'I haven't
had much time, you know.'

'Well, if you could give us any information at all,' said Jamie. 'Anything that would help.'

Carla and Pedro didn't say anything, which made me feel a bit guilty. After all, I was the one who'd got this man involved. However, if he could help us, I reasoned to myself, then all would have been worthwhile.

The man wrapped a gnarled hand around the half glass of beer he was nursing. He swirled the contents around, making the remains of the head settle on top of the beer that was left. Slowly and deliberately. Then he took a deep gulp. I wanted to shake him, but I figured he was not one to be rushed. We waited until he put down the glass and wiped his mouth with the back of his hand.

Then he looked at us. 'Name's Pete,' he said. 'Who are you all?'

Oh lord, would he ever get on to the important bit? It was Jamie who introduced us all. Pete's interest focused on Carla and Pedro. 'So, you've come from Spain to look for this...this treasure, have you?'

Pedro shuffled and gave a sickly smile. 'It's just ... just something that turned up in the family history,' he said. 'A story that has been passed from generation to generation. There might not even be any truth in it...'

'And what would that story be?' put in Pete. 'There's all kinds of stories that have been passed from generation to generation. What might yours be?'

Carla and Pedro glanced at one another, but neither of them seemed prepared to speak.

'For heaven's sake!' I burst out. This cat and mouse game was driving me daft. 'It's nothing to be ashamed of. Look,' I turned to Pete, 'it's very simple. At the time of the Battle of Kinsale, some Spanish ships sailed into ... into...'

'Into Castlehaven,' prompted Jamie.

'That's the one,' I continued. 'They came to help the O'Driscolls fight the English.'

Pete was nodding. 'A failed coup,' he said. 'The ships were sunk.'

I was amazed. 'You know about that?'

He laughed, his leathery tan wrinkling deeply. 'It's a well known story. Donogh O'Driscoll, of Castlehaven castle, secretly arranged for six Spanish ships to sail into Castlehaven to help the O'Driscolls hold on to their land.'

'Was that the Spanish Armada?' asked Leo.

'Don't be daft,' I sniggered. 'That was ages before. That Drake man with the tights and fluffy collar was playing marbles when the Spanish Armada sailed into *England*, you twit. Nothing to do with Ireland.'

Jamie smiled and shook his head. 'The Spanish Armada was actually 1588,' he said. 'Just a few years before the Battle of Kinsale. And Sir Francis Drake was playing bowls.'

'Whatever. Who cares?' I muttered. I really hate it when people show off, especially when it makes me look a prat. I sniffed and turned to Pete. 'So, what happened then?'

'They were attacked by an Admiral Levison,' he went on. 'He sank some of the ships and rounded up the rest. Later on, after the Battle of Kinsale – a terrible disaster for Cork – the O'Driscolls were stripped of their castle and all their possessions. They had to flee the country.'

'The Flight of the Earls,' I said. I remembered this bit of history because I used to imagine what it would be like to flee with a hunky earl way back then. The thoughts of being smuggled aboard one of those galleon things in the

dead of night with a black cape covering my rustling silk dress brightened up several dreary history classes.

Pete nodded. 'That's right,' he said, visibly impressed by my scholarly input. 'But what's your end of the story?'

'One of the Spanish captains was the ancestor of Carla and Pedro here,' said Jamie. 'He was sheltered by the O'Driscolls because the English were searching for the survivors....'

'But he had to run away in case he was betrayed,' interrupted Leo.

'And obviously, from what you've just told us, before the castle was confiscated,' added Jamie.

'He had to hide his present in case he was nicked,' Leo interrupted again.

Pete's attention switched to Leo. 'Present?' he asked.

There was no stopping Leo now. 'Yes. The head of the O'Driscoll clan gave him a present for trying to chase the English away. Something very valuable. A treasure. And that's what Carla and Pedro are looking for. It belongs to them.' Leo sat back, looking very pleased with himself.

Anyone would think it had been him and not me who got this whole thing rolling.

Nobody said anything for what seemed like ages. You could see Pete running the information through the mind under the woolly hat. At length he looked across at Carla and Pedro who were sitting close together, still with their mouths firmly clamped shut.

'And have you anything to go on?' asked Pete.

'The letter!' cried Leo. 'Show him the letter, Pedro.'

Reluctantly, Pedro took the letter from his pocket. You could see that he was mortified at being identified with this whole weird story. But at least it was out in the open now and we might get help. Pete's face became very serious as he glanced over the contents of the now tattered translation of the letter.

'This is all you have to go on?' he asked. Pedro nodded. 'Tisn't a lot, is it?' observed Pete.

'It's a start,' I put in, just to make Pedro feel a bit better. Pete was shaking his head.

'I couldn't make head nor tail of this myself,' he said. 'Do you mind if I just write it down? If I look at it when I've more time, I might come up with an answer.'

Pedro was biting his lip. I could see he was anxious to get the letter back.

Jamie looked over at Pedro, sensing his doubt. 'Is that

all right?' he asked. 'It's worth a try. Pete might just be able to get the information we want.'

'What's in it for you?' Pedro asked Pete. Bit cheeky, I thought.

But Pete took it good-naturedly. He laughed and offered the letter back to Pedro. 'Nothing at all, son,' he said. 'Nothing in it for me. Just trying to be helpful, that's all.'

Pedro looked contrite. 'Sorry,' he said. 'Sure, if you think it would help, copy down the translation. Anything you come up with will help.'

Pete produced a pencil and notebook from his pocket and proceeded to copy out the letter.

'We were thinking of going to Castletownshend,' said Jamie. 'There's an O'Driscoll castle there and it's near where the Spanish flotilla came in...'

Pete was shaking his head as he mulled over what he'd just written. 'You don't want to go there,' he said. 'You won't find anything there.' He looked up at us as he put the sheet of paper into his pocket. 'Where you want to go is Sherkin.'

'Sherkin Island?' asked Jamie.

'That's the one,' said Pete. 'That was an O'Driscoll stronghold. That would have been an ideal place for a fugitive to hide. You want to get yourselves to Sherkin. Look out for an old fellow there, name of McCaffrey. He lives in the third cottage beyond the church. You can't miss it. He should be able to help you.'

'How do we get to...?' began Leo.

'The ferry,' said Pete. He looked at his watch. 'The next ferry leaves at twelve. Bring a picnic and make a day of it. Ye can bring your bikes on the ferry,' he added helpfully. He got up. 'Have to go now. Lobster pots to put out. If I get any more information, I'll let ye know. Where are ye staying?'

'We're staying in a house up a lane...' began Leo. But Pete was looking at Pedro.

'Yourself,' he said. 'Whereabouts are you staying so that I'll know where to find you?'

'The hostel,' muttered Pedro. 'We're staying at the hostel.'

'Grand,' said Pete. 'Well, the best of luck. I'll keep in touch.' And he was gone down to his van which had lobsters and fish painted on the sides.

We watched him drive off, giving us a cheery wave as he passed. We looked at one another, nobody quite knowing what to say.

'Well,' I said eventually, 'this could be the solution to our problem. We might find what we want on Sherkin. It's a start.' I was trying to sound optimistic.

At long last Pedro spoke up. 'It might,' he said. There was doubt in his tone of voice.

'What are you thinking?' asked Jamie. 'Don't you trust him?'

Pedro shrugged. 'I suppose it can't do any harm,' he said. 'What have we to lose?'

But the look that passed between himself and Carla told me that there was an awful lot to lose if this search proved fruitless. Like, cheap wine flooding Europe and their Spanish Da in the workhouse gnashing his gums and talking about the good old days. At this stage I was determined not to let that happen.

We picked up some crisps, cheese, ham and orange in the shop. Then we went down to the harbour and waited for the ferry to Sherkin.

11

The Search on Sherkin

The ferry was packed with day trippers. Once our bikes were stored, I dragged Leo to the back of the boat.

'What are you doing?' he wailed as I gripped his arm. 'I want to stay up front.'

I gritted my teeth. 'Listen,' I said. 'For once will you not be so selfish. Just stick with me. Can you do that?'

Realisation dawned on him. 'Oh no,' he groaned. 'You're never going to throw up again, are you?'

But he sat down beside me, to give him his due. The engine throbbed to life and we were off. Already the blood was draining from my face and my stomach was taking a nasty turn. I concentrated on the V-shaped track the ferry was leaving in the water and tried to think positive thoughts. But the only positive thought that I could come up with was that I was positively going to see my breakfast again very soon.

'Don't look at the water,' a voice murmured. I turned to see Jamie standing beside me. He'd made his way through the crowded boat to me. I didn't know whether to be delighted or to feel even more panicky. Bad enough to have my cousin witness my green death, but I certainly didn't want Jamie to see me like this.

'Look at the land,' he went on. 'Concentrate on the land and you'll be fine. Take a deep breath.'

I took a gulp of air and didn't fall apart. We passed near the big yacht and I concentrated on seeing if there were any mega-stars on board. There was just one person messing about on the deck, an oldish guy in a red and white striped tee-shirt. The man Carla and I had been waving to. If I'd known he was old I'd have saved my energy. He looked up as the ferry passed, but didn't wave. In fact he quickly disappeared into the cabin. He could have been nipping down to tell Bono or Brad Pitt or someone that there was a load of riff-raff passing and not to show their faces in case they'd be mobbed.

Jamie pointed out the beacon where Carla and I had been. He kept up a running commentary to keep my mind off my churning stomach.

'You did it!' said Leo suddenly. 'We're there and you didn't throw up.'

Sure enough, the engine slowed to a hum and we were drawing into the small harbour at Sherkin. The gulls wheeled and dived alongside. Their beady eyes seemed to be looking straight at me, waiting for me to make a fool of myself. But, thanks to Jamie, I was okay.

'Thanks,' I said.

'For nothing,' he grinned.

Carla and Pedro, who'd been to the front of the ferry, were first out. They seemed to be arguing in Spanish, but they stopped and smiled as we reached them.

'All set then?' said Pedro.

We mounted our bikes and set off across the island, not quite knowing where we were going, but following Pete's directions.

'Cycling is for nutters and health freaks,' I panted as I tried to keep up with the others, swerving in and out to avoid knocking off the day trippers who were on foot. 'And who left all these cruddy hills lying about?'

Jamie dismounted and laughed as he waited for me to catch up. 'Come on, Maeve,' he said. 'We're nearly there. Look, you can see the church at the top of that hill.'

'Not another stupid hill,' I groaned. 'My legs were made for better things than this.'

Leo, Pedro and Carla were standing at a rusty, crooked gate outside a dilapidated cottage .

'This is the third cottage from the church,' said Leo with a certain amount of doubt in his voice. 'But it doesn't look like anyone lives here.'

'Maybe he's just a messy old fogey who doesn't care what his house looks like,' I said. 'Maybe the inside is fine.'

'Well, we're here so we might as well get on with it,' said Pedro. He leaned his bike against the wall and pushed open the gate. It squeaked in protest, giving further doubt to habitation. The rest of us waited while Pedro knocked on the door. He knocked again, then turned towards us, shrugging his shoulders.

'Who are you looking for?' The voice startled us. An old man with a sheep-dog emerged from a field beside us.

'Are you Mr McCaffrey?' asked Jamie.

The man threw back his head and laughed, revealing acres of gum and a couple of courageous teeth that were hanging on against all the odds. 'Is it Jack McCaffrey you want?' he asked.

'I think so,' said Jamie. 'All we know is that he lives in this cottage.'

'Hmmmppff,' said the man. He'd reached us now and was leaning against the wall. He looked up as Pedro joined us again. 'And what would you be wanting Jack McCaffrey for?'

'We were told that he might be able to tell us...to tell us something of historic interest,' said Jamie.

We waited expectantly for the old man to tell us where

we might find Jack McCaffrey.

But, like everyone else around here, he had problems with getting to the point.

'And who was it told you this?' he asked.

'A man called Pete,' put in Leo. 'In Baltimore.'

'Is it Pete the lobster fisherman?' the man asked.

I felt like crying out, *What does it matter which cruddy Pete it is? Just tell us where we'll find this old geezer so that we can get on with our business.* But Grandpa Gummy was not to be rushed.

'I wonder now,' he muttered. 'I wonder why he sent you to Jack McCaffrey.' He chewed his gums while he pondered on this.

'He told us that Mr McCaffrey was an authority on local history,' said Jamie patiently.

'He did? Ha!' More gum chewing.

'Can you please tell us where he lives?' asked Pedro. 'We'd like very much to speak to him.'

The old man looked with interest at Pedro. 'You foreign?' he asked.

I bit my fist to stop the groan that was fighting its way from my mouth. Would we have to resort to torture to find out what we wanted to know?

Pedro nodded. 'Yes,' he said, without offering any further information. This old fogey had probably never heard of Spain anyway.

'About Jack McCaffrey,' prompted Jamie.

'What? Oh yes. Jack. Poor old Jack. He's above in the graveyard. That's where Jack is.' Then he laughed his disgusting gummy laugh again.

'Is he the caretaker?' asked Carla. You could see that she was losing her patience too.

The man looked at her for another gum-gnashing moment before chortling again.

'Caretaker? Oh no, no. Sure poor old Jack died five years ago. The rheumatics got him in the end. Them and the fags.'

'He's dead?' said Leo. 'He can't be. There must be another Mr McCaffrey. Pete said...'

'That fellow is playing a trick on you,' laughed the old man. 'Old Jack was the only McCaffrey on Sherkin island. Sure Pete knows as well as myself that Jack is gone to his reward. He was at the funeral. He's having you on.' He rambled off, chuckling as he went.

Pedro kicked at the grass on the side of the road. 'We've been fooled,' he said.

'But why?' asked Leo. 'Why would Pete want to make fools of us? It's not the least bit funny.'

'I don't think it was meant to be funny,' said Pedro.

'What do you mean?' asked Carla.

Pedro was frowning. 'I never really trusted him,' he said.

'You could be right,' agreed Jamie. 'He made a great show of being helpful but, if you think about it, all he did was ask us lots of questions.'

A sudden thought occurred to me. Pete had taken down the translation of the Spanish letter. I swallowed hard, feeling I was responsible for all this. Which I was, really.

Please let them not remember that he has the words of the letter, I prayed.

'He has the letter!' exclaimed Leo. I should have known the little darling would land me in it. 'He copied the letter!'

'He'd never work it out,' I stammered. 'He's too thick. It will be okay. He must have made a mistake. I'm sure he means well...' my voice trailed off as four taut faces looked at me. I was barking up the wrong tree, there was no doubt about that. Trouble, Maeve.

'Maybe he's right about the castle,' said Jamie. Loyal friend rushing to save my bacon. 'Let's find out if there's an O'Driscoll castle on the island.'

We cycled to a shop and four of us waited while Jamie went in to inquire. Nobody said anything, but I knew I was not flavour of the month.

Never again, I swore, never again would I try to help anyone. Especially not foreigners with cock-eyed stories about half-witted ancestors who couldn't look after a simple bag of goodies.

THE BUNGLING MARINER

By Maeve Morris

With tear-filled eye and trembling lip
The sailor jumped his Spanish ship.
It upped and hit a granite rock.
'Ole!' he cried. 'Me ship's a crock.
I'd better hide my Spanish face.
Before Queen Bessie's men give chase.'

We couldn't tell from Jamie's expression whether the news was good or bad.

'There *is* an O'Driscoll castle here,' he said.

'Great!' said Leo. But Jamie was shaking his head.

'We can't get into it,' he said. 'It's cordoned off by the Board of Public Works. They're working at restoring it. No one is allowed inside.'

'Let's ask,' I said. 'Tell them we won't do any harm.'

Jamie shrugged and looked at Pedro.

'At least we could see where it is,' said Pedro.

We followed the road to where hoarding and scaffolding surrounded a ruined abbey and, nearby, the castle we were looking for. Several men with plastic hats were shuffling around. They looked up when we approached.

'Excuse me,' said Jamie in his most polite fashion. 'Do you think we could have a look at the castle?'

From their expressions you would think he'd asked them to surrender their tools and hand over the whole ancient pile to us.

The most authoritative looking one (wearing a suit) finally found his voice. 'Oh no, lad,' he laughed. 'No visitors allowed. Not until we've restored it and made it safe.'

'But we just want a quick look,' went on Jamie.

'We will not be long,' put in Carla, dazzling the hard hats with her smile. 'Please?'

But all the dazzle and politeness were to no avail. The man was adamant. There was power in that plastic hat and he was intent on using it.

'Sorry, love,' he said. 'Insurance and all that. If any of you got hurt we'd all be without a job.'

There was no arguing with that. We slunk away.

'Maybe we could come back when they've gone,' I said. 'Wait until they lock up...'

Then Jamie gave a sudden whoop and handed his bike to Leo before dashing back to where the men were working.

'I've told you, kid...' began Mr Bossman.

'The castle,' Jamie cut across him. 'Can you tell me when it became a ruin?'

The man lifted his hat and scratched his balding head. 'I can,' he said. 'It was built in 1460 and destroyed in the mid 1500s.'

'Thanks,' Jamie shouted and ran back to the rest of us who were looking at him quizzically.

'Just as I thought,' he said. 'This castle was a ruin long before Don Pedro came to Ireland. He couldn't have stayed here. We can definitely rule out this castle.'

Well that certainly put a dampener on our spirits. Any hope I might have had of exonerating myself was well and truly banished.

12

Lightning Storm and the Legend of Labhras

We cycled to a beach and ate our picnic. Nobody felt much like talking, but we were stuck here until the next ferry so we had to make the most of it. Leo found an old, burst football and we kicked it around. We ended up having so much fun that we almost forgot about rotten Pete sending us here on a wild-goose chase. We threw ourselves on to the sand, exhausted. It was only then that I noticed my legs. The front of my thighs and shins were bright pink. Hot, burning, bright pink.

'Oh cripes!' I muttered. 'I'm sunburnt.'

'Poor Maeve,' said Carla sympathetically. 'You should have worn sun-block. With your fair skin you need to protect it.'

I glanced at her deep tan and scowled.

'You're like a lobster,' laughed Leo. 'Your forehead and nose are burnt too.'

I felt my hot forehead, visualising its angry pink colour.

'Cruddy bike,' I said. 'This is what comes of cruddy cycling.'

'Mum has sun cream at home,' said Jamie. 'You can put it on when we get back.'

Great, I thought. *Here's another reason for Mumsy to cast her evil eye on me. Not alone do I throw up, I also sizzle like a crisp rasher in the sun. More ammunition for her disapproval. Please, please let herself and her stupid yacht be carried out to sea. The Caribbean Sea. For several weeks.*

Pedro was idly drawing on the sand with a stick.

'That looks like a castle,' observed Leo. 'Are you

drawing a castle, Pedro?'

Pedro sighed and threw the stick away. 'Just scribbling,' he said. 'Thinking of castles in general, I suppose.'

'You're thinking about Pete, aren't you?' went on Leo.

God, wasn't I in enough pain without dragging all this up again?

'Yes,' agreed Pedro. 'I'm wondering what his game is.'

'Maybe he doesn't know that the castle here is the wrong one,' I said. 'Maybe he thought he was pointing in the right direction.'

Pedro shook his head. 'It was too blatant,' he said. 'He was too quick to suggest this place. It just does not ring true.'

'You think he might be after the treasure himself?' asked Jamie. 'Do you really think he could work out the riddle of that letter?'

'That's what worries me,' said Pedro.

'No,' said Carla. 'Surely not. Surely he couldn't work it out.'

'I should not have let him copy that letter,' groaned Pedro. 'That was not clever.'

'We could ask for it back,' said Leo.

Pedro gave him a sort of scathing look. 'And you think he would oblige? He's already made fools of us, he's hardly likely to ...'

'We should never have even talked to him,' burst out Carla. 'That was a mistake.'

'I just thought he'd help,' I put in. It was time to put up the defences. 'I really thought he might be able to give us some help – being local and all that.'

'You should have kept your mouth shut,' said Leo. 'That's your trouble, Maeve. You barge right in...'

'Stop!' said Jamie. 'We're not going to get anywhere

snapping and accusing. We'll just have to be watchful and try to stay one step ahead of Pete. Look, when we get back to the house, we'll pore over the letter and see if there's even one small thing that will give us a lead. In the meantime,' he looked at his watch. 'In the meantime we should be heading back for the ferry.'

I smiled at him gratefully. Once again he'd taken the heat off me. Heat! I bit my lip as I struggled up, my legs screaming in agony. Here was another heat I wished he could lift. Never again would I subject an innocent slice of bread to the torture of being toasted.

I was so sore and miserable on the way back that I quite forgot about the waves that rocked the ferry. When we got to Baltimore, Jamie suggested that Pedro and Carla come back with us and we'd make supper. He rooted about in his mother's stuff and produced a bottle of expensive (the astronomical price was still on it) *après-sun* lotion. It said on the label that it was also soothing for *après-ski* sunburn. Now *that* was handy to know, I thought as I slathered it over all my burnt bits.

Downstairs the lights were full on, even though it was only early evening. The sky had suddenly darkened as an ominous cloud hovered over the whole bay. Mount Gabriel was completely blotted out, as was Sherkin.

'We're in for one hell of a storm,' said Jamie, looking out anxiously.

'I hope your folks are safe,' said Leo.

I gulped guiltily and wondered if my wish for a mishap to his mother had anything to do with it. Was there witchcraft in my ancestry? Then Jamie laughed and turned from the window. 'They're too experienced to let a thunderstorm drive them off course,' he said, as if he'd read my mind. 'They've survived worse than this in bigger seas. Come on, let's have a look at that letter and see if we can come up with any further meaning.'

We pored over it again, but nobody had anything more to offer. The sky outside grew darker and the rumble of thunder drew nearer. Out in the bay the water became choppy and the moored yachts tossed about like birthday candles on jelly. As the others watched in fascination, every now and then uttering in awe as a lightning flash cracked the heavy clouds, I wandered over to the bookshelves. The sight of all those boats bobbing about was bad for my health.

I idly picked up a book entitled *West Cork, Fact and Legend*. Sitting with my back to the action outside, I ran my finger down the index. O'Driscoll was listed. There were pages and pages of information on the O'Driscolls. Why did there have to be so darn many of them? I mused. I flicked through the pages to see if there were any pictures, and came to a drawing of a castle on an island. At first I thought it was Sherkin – to me one chunk of land surrounded by water is much the same as another – but underneath it said 'Cloghan Castle, Lough Hyne (an early O'Driscoll castle)'. There was a legend about the place and I settled down to read it, trying to ignore the rumbles and flashes.

It was a weird story about some old guy called Labhras O'Loinseach, or Labhras *Dá Cluai*s as he became known, who lived in this castle. His fiancée popped her clogs and, in his grief, he married her sister. This sister was a bit of a dragon, bit like Jamie's mother, I sniggered to myself. Anyway, the dead fiancée appeared to Labhras and told him to scarper from the evil wife and the island, that things could get hairy if he hung around.

But before he could pack toothbrush and pyjamas, the new wife muscled in and asked him where he was off to. When she heard he was running out on her she exploded with rage, caught him by the ears and swung him round her head. Needless to say this caused severe stretching of the ears, pulling them out of all proportion. So poor old Labhras was lumbered with sticky-up ears that made him look like a donkey. Well, that certainly kept him on the island. You don't want to be wandering around ancient Ireland with lugs like a donkey. This presented a bit of a problem haircut-wise. He couldn't just wander into your average barber, plonk himself on the high chair and ask for a short back and sides.

So, the upshot of this was that he'd rent a barber who did house-calls, ferry him to the island and then, when the hair was trimmed and the last bit of gel patted into place, Labhras would have the unfortunate barber done in.

Well one day barber number one-hundred-and-one was ferried over. He was a bit surprised when, instead of the price of the haircut, he was confronted by some ancient Arnold Schwarzenegger wielding a hatchet. The poor geezer pleaded that his ma was sick and that if he was rubbed out, she'd have no one to care for her.

Labhras was touched. He'd often wished his own old

mammy was around to put manners on the amazon of a wife. He told the barber that he'd spare him so long as he swore never to breathe a word about the weird ears to a living soul. The barber agreed, as you would, considering the gory alternative. However, the barber was a bit of a wimp. The burden of the secret was driving him loopy. So, one day he whispered the secret to an oak-tree.

'You won't believe this, O Oak-Tree,' he said. 'But that crazy Labhras O'Loinseach has donkey's ears.' Why that should have made him feel better I don't know.

Anyway, he cut down the oak-tree and had a harp made from the wood. This eventually came into the possession of a harper who made his living by giving gigs in castles. Needless to say he was invited to warble a tune in Labhras's castle. Neighbours gathered in the big hall, as excited as a mob at the Point for a pop concert. Labhras, his hair curled nicely around the big ears, sat on his throne feeling like a top dog. The harper cleared his throat, tested a few strings and began to play. But the harp took on a life of its own and began to sing, 'Labhras O'Loinseach has donkey's ears. Labhras O'Loinseach has donkey's ears.'

That got the crowd going. Poor old Labhras got such a shock that he fell back, dead as a dodo. Bit unfair, I thought. But then, if you rub out barbers I suppose you have to get some kind of come-uppance. Thank goodness I'd refrained from doing in the old bat who'd tortured my hair.

Hold on! A sudden thought occurred to me.

I read back over the story, hardly daring to breathe. No, it couldn't be. Surely I was going as loopy as old Labhras. But as I glanced over the words I'd been reading, I felt as if a fog was clearing from my brain.

13

My Next Brilliant Deduction

'HEY!' I spluttered. The others looked over at me. 'The letter!' I exclaimed. 'Let me see the letter.'

'It's there, on the table where we left it,' said Jamie with surprise. 'What are you at?'

But I'd dashed across to the table and snatched up the letter. 'I have it!' I gasped. 'I've worked it out.'

'What!' the other four gathered around.

'I know which castle we're looking for,' I went on. I put down the book and pointed to the legend I'd just been reading. Jamie took the book and began to read aloud: '*The Legend of Labhras O'Loinseach,*' he began. He looked at me with a puzzled expression. 'I don't see what...'

'Go on,' I urged him.

He started to read again. I waited patiently until he'd finished. He put down the book and gave me another puzzled look, as did Carla and Pedro. Leo had turned the book around so that he could see it and was running his finger along the words.

'Ha!' he exclaimed triumphantly. '*Dhá cluais!* That's it!'

The other three still didn't get it.

'Ears,' I explained, remembering that none of them knew any Irish. Leo and I were the only ones who did. '*Cluais* is the Irish for ears. Don't you see? Here in the letter it says; "You must seek the cast ... scoll. The legend ... Labh ... a cluais ... Seek the stone that bears the emblem ... arp of barb ... waters that gush..."'

Leo was jumping up and down with excitement. 'We

100

have it, we have it,' he was shouting. 'Look,' he put the letter beside the passage in the book. I let him talk. I was too excited to trust my own speech. 'Listen,' he went on: '"You must seek the cast*le of O'Dri*scoll. The legend *of* Labh*ras* D*há Cluais.* Seek the stone that bears the emblem ... *h*arp of barber..."'

'The emblem with the *harp*!' Jamie interrupted him excitedly. 'Good lord! You're right.'

'And there's even a picture of the castle,' I put in. 'It's called Cloghan Castle and it's on Lough Hyne.'

'Lough Hyne is only a few miles away,' said Jamie.

Now it was Carla and Pedro's turn to get excited. They began to talk animatedly to one another in Spanish. When they became aware of the rest of us looking at them, Carla laughed.

'Sorry,' she said. 'We just can't believe that things are working out so well. We're so lucky that we told you.'

I waited for someone to tell me how wonderful I was. Would I have to point it out myself? It always takes the good out of it if you have to blow your own trumpet.

It was Pedro who leaned towards me. 'Well done, Maeve,' he said. 'You're very clever. Amazing!'

Could I have that in writing? I wanted to cry out. I felt my face blushing, but then I realised that nobody would notice the blush – my face was already bright pink with sunburn.

Jamie was also looking at me with admiration. 'Good on you, Maeve,' he grinned.

Carla clapped me on the back, a gesture which painfully made me realise that that area was burnt as well. No matter. What was a bit of suffering when people were heaping honours on my head.

Pedro was now poring over the letter. 'So,' he said.

'We'll go to this castle on Lough Hyne...'

'It's probably a ruin,' said Jamie. 'But, so what. It's definitely the castle that Don Pedro wanted his descendants to go to. He might not necessarily have stayed there, but he used it for the purpose of hiding whatever it was he wanted to protect. There are bound to be enough remains to reveal something.'

'And the "waters that gush",' Carla said. 'What could that be?'

We looked at one another for inspiration.

'Beats me.' Jamie shrugged his shoulders. I didn't know either, but I felt I'd done my bit at this stage.

'Hey,' said Leo. 'I've just thought of something. If this ruin is on an island, how do we get across to it?'

'The dinghy,' I said. 'The dinghy that's moored on the shingle beach.'

But Jamie was shaking his head. 'We've no way of transporting it to Lough Hyne,' he said. Then he began to grin. 'But there's an inflatable out in the garage.'

'A what?' I asked.

'A blow-up boat,' explained Leo.

'With an outboard motor,' went on Jamie. 'We're okay. We'll manage those on the bikes.'

'This is great,' said Pedro at last. 'But let's not get too excited. Remember these instructions were written out centuries ago. There might be no trace of any of these things.'

Carla said something in Spanish that sounded very angry. Then she turned towards the rest of us. 'Don't mind him,' she said. 'He's just being a grouch.'

'Just being realistic,' said Pedro. 'I don't want us getting all excited and then being let down. Let's just take it one step at a time, eh?'

'Yes. I suppose you're right,' said Jamie. 'Still,' he added, brightening up. 'It's great that we have so much information. At least we know where to look.'

'When?' asked Leo, hopping about again. 'When will we go there?'

The storm was still raging outside and there was no sign of it letting up. 'Let's eat while we sit out the storm,' suggested Jamie.

Carla offered to make us a Spanish omelette. She chopped up tomatoes and onions and some other stuff and mixed it all in with the eggs that Leo whipped. Pedro sat in the window-seat, examining the letter and the story. Every now and then he'd write something on a piece of paper which he stuffed into his pocket when the meal was ready.

'I suppose he's writing it all down in his own language,' whispered Jamie as he helped me to set the table. Well, that certainly made sense. We sat around the big table and Carla dished out the slices of omelette. I was starving.

'Looks good, Carla,' said Jamie.

'Smashing,' said Leo.

Gross, I thought. I nudged Leo while the others were talking. 'Remind me not to go to Spain,' I whispered. 'Not if this is the sort of muck they eat. No wonder their ships sank.' Leo spluttered into his napkin and vanished under the table in a fit of sniggering.

'Don't mind him,' I said innocently to the others.'He's just a kid with no manners.'

Day turned to evening. Every so often one of us would wander over to the window to see if there was any sign of the weather improving. Now that we had a direction for our search, we were all anxious to get on with it. The thunder and lightning had long since ceased, but the rain had settled into a steady drizzle. Not weather for shuffling about ruined castles.

By the time it did improve, it was night. 'Typical,' I said. 'Why couldn't the rain decide to shove off a bit earlier so that we could get out?'

'How about we go into the village,' said Pedro.

'That sounds good,' I replied. A bit of action would be welcome.

The air smelled fresh after all the rain. The fuchsia bushes were still dripping as we made our way down the hill into the brightly lit village. Once more there were crowds congregating on the square above the harbour. The noisy chat and laughter were welcome after being shut up in the house.

'What's everybody having?' asked Pedro. 'My grateful treat.' When he'd got the order for Coke and crisps and orange, Jamie and I wandered down to the harbour to look at the boats while Carla and Leo chatted about matters Spanish.

'I love this place,' said Jamie as we left the noise behind us and walked along the almost deserted pier. Now all we could hear was the gentle clang of the masts on the yachts. 'I'm really glad my folks switched with the Jacksons... You were great to work out that letter,' he added, turning towards me.

'Just a bit of luck,' I said dismissively. 'Just happened to pick up the right book. It was a chance in a million.'

It's easy to feign modesty when you've proved your genius.

'No, you were on the ball,' he said. 'You very quickly spotted the connection.' He grinned, his teeth white in the gloom. 'So, how is the holiday going now? Am I still a prat?'

We both laughed. But before I had time to answer, the sound of a mobile phone ringing reached us from away out across the water. 'A phone out here!' I laughed. 'Some mermaid ringing for a takeaway?'

'Sound carries across the water,' explained Jamie. 'It must be a mobile on one of those yachts.'

'It has to be the big one,' I said. 'It's the only one with lights on. It's probably Brad Pitt's agent telling him about his next film. Probably telling him to look out for a beautiful young girl to play the lead female role. Should I swim out there, do you think?'

Jamie laughed. 'You're crazy, Maeve Morris,' he said. 'This holiday just wouldn't be any fun without you.'

'Tell that to Brad Pitt,' I laughed and ran back towards the harbour.

Carla and Leo were still chatting. Carla looked up and

smiled when she saw us coming. 'Can't think what's keeping Pedro,' she said, glancing towards the pub.

It took about another ten minutes for Pedro to return with the drinks. 'What kept you?' asked Leo. 'Did you have to peel the spuds for the crisps yourself?'

'Sorry,' said Pedro, putting the glasses down in front of us. 'Big crowd.' Then he leaned towards us. 'Guess who's inside?' he went on.

'Brad?' I said. 'Johnny Depp? Keanu Reeves?'

'Our friend Pete?' said Jamie.

Pedro nodded. 'Along with that fellow who shunted us out of the castle. They're deep in conversation. I was watching them.'

'Let's go in and tackle him over sending us on the wrong trail,' said Leo, hopping down from his seat. Action Man with knobbly knees ready to take on the enemy. 'Tell him he's a crooked...'

'No,' said Pedro. 'Don't even go in there. We don't want them to know we're on to them. Just play it cool.'

'You're right,' agreed Jamie. 'No point in drawing them on us.'

The night passed pleasantly. A long-haired guy wearing Jesus sandals and sawn-off shorts plucked at his guitar and soon everyone on the square was joining in old Beatles numbers and Irish ballads – the sort of stuff I'd normally scoff at back in the real world. I was sitting beside Pedro and every now and then he'd grin at me as he tried to keep up with the words. Once or twice I noticed Jamie looking in my direction which did no end of good to my ego. If this was being a *femme fatale*, well I resolved there and then that femme fataling was pretty cool.

'Old Brad doesn't know what he's missing,' I said,

nodding towards the big yacht which was well lit up.

'What?' said Pedro.

'Brad Pitt or Bono or whatever big shot is hiding his face out there in that big tub. Wouldn't they be better off to come in and join the fun.'

Pedro laughed and said something to Carla who laughed also. I wished I knew Spanish. It's not nice having your scintillating wit translated when you don't know how well it's being translated.

'Dream on, Maeve,' said Leo. 'It's probably some boring old geezer who hates fun.'

'Boring old geezers don't tend to have boats ... yachts like that great monster,' I retorted.

Pedro was looking at his watch. 'Half past eleven,' he announced, giving Leo a playful dig in the ribs. 'Too late for small boys to be out. Let's go.'

We were half way up the hill when Leo decided he wanted to go to the loo. 'I'll just be a sec,' he said.

'You shouldn't drink so much orange,' laughed Carla.

But Pedro caught Leo and swung him playfully over his shoulder. 'Not likely, old son,' he laughed. 'You just want to go back there and take on those two prats. You'd end up in jail for causing GBH.'

'What's GBH?' asked Leo.

'Grievous bodily harm,' put in Jamie. 'If we let you loose on those guys they'd end up in traction and we'd be visiting you in the nick. You wouldn't like the nick, Leo. Hairy bacon and watery veg.'

Pedro suddenly looked serious. 'Let's get out to that island early in the morning,' he said. 'Just in case those two succeed in working something out from the letter.'

That certainly gave us major food for thought for the night.

14

The Chase Begins

Leo had us up at cock-crow next morning. 'Leo, it's only half past eight,' I groaned.

'We've got to get to that castle before Pete and his side-kick,' he replied. 'If they find that treasure thing, Carla and Pedro's father will lose his vineyard. Think of someone else besides yourself for a change,' he added scornfully before nipping back to the safety of his room.

I gritted my teeth. Bad enough to have to crawl out of bed at this unearthly hour without having insults thrown in. Wasn't the little prat forgetting that I was the one who'd worked out the whole solution?

Jamie was yawning as he poured out his cornflakes. He grinned when he saw me coming downstairs. The jeans I was wearing were rubbing painfully against my sunburnt thighs, in spite of Lady Corduroy's expensive cream. I made a mental note to change into leggings before we left. I tried not to think of the peeling nose.

'The things we do for friendship,' he said.

'You've said it,' I replied. 'Maybe they'll fly us out to their vineyard when this is over. I could do with a spot of pampering as a reward. Spanish servants who'll respond to my every whim. Galloping around the vast estate with Pedro on white chargers ... Only kidding,' I added when I saw Leo's look of disgust.

Pedro and Carla appeared just as we were stacking our dishes into the sink. Pedro gleefully pointed to a small trailer which was attached to his bike. 'Borrowed it from a Norwegian chap at the hostel,' he explained.

'Terrific, Pedro,' said Jamie. 'It will take the inflatable and the motor easily.'

'Do we need the life-jackets?' asked Leo.

Jamie thought for a moment. 'No,' he said. 'It's only a short distance across to the island. We'll be over in five minutes.'

Leo gave me an anxious look. Last thing our folks had warned us about was to wear a life-jacket at all times out on the water. Heck, I thought, Jamie must know best. I shrugged and nodded to Leo who seemed relieved.

So we set off. There was very little traffic on the road at that hour. Just as well because there were so many twists and turns you could splat on to an oncoming car if you took an extra centimetre towards the middle of the road.

We were just coming to a big fish warehouse sort of place when we saw Pete's distinctive van parked inside the gates. He was loading boxes of fish into the back of the van. 'Hello, there,' he shouted, cool as you like. 'Where are you all heading at this hour?'

'Mind your own...' I began.

'Ballydehob,' put in Jamie. 'We're going to Bally-dehob.'

'I want to talk to you,' Pete called out. 'About that letter...'

'Later,' shouted Jamie. 'Catch you later.'

'Hold on,' yelled Pete, waving his arms. But we pretended not to hear and kept on going.

'What do you think he wanted?' asked Carla when we were out of Pete's line of vision.

'To send us astray again, no doubt,' said Pedro.

'More than likely,' agreed Jamie. 'Smarmy so and so.'

'Well, at least we know he's not searching for Don Pedro's stuff,' I said. 'That's a relief.'

We continued on our tortuous journey. Every turn of the pedals made my sunburnt legs sing in agony, but at least the wind kept them cool through my leggings. We stopped at a crossroads and Jamie produced a map. 'That's Knockomagh ahead,' he said, pointing to a hill.

'We don't have to cycle up that thing, do we?' I asked.

Jamie laughed. 'No,' he said. 'The lake is just under it. We're pretty close now.'

I groaned as we mounted up again. All this physical activity was playing havoc with my health. I could understand now why joggers and cyclists always look so totally miserable.

THE CHEERLESS CYCLIST

By Maeve Morris

His knobbly knees go round and round.
His little heart begins to pound.
He never stops to draw a breath,
Although his lungs are screaming 'Death!'
There is no need for all this strife.
Why can't he simply get a life!

We had just rounded a bend when we heard an engine behind us. We spread out into single file to let the vehicle pass. I nearly fell off my bike when I recognised Pete's van. Was there no end to the man's cheek?

He lowered the passenger window as he drew level. 'You're going the wrong way to Ballydehob,' he shouted.

'We're taking the scenic route,' Pedro called back.

'I think I might have some more information for you about that legend,' went on Pete, his van keeping pace with us.

I was tempted to shout something very meaningful, but I figured Pedro was the one who'd come up with the right response.

'The legend?' He pretended to be surprised. 'Oh, we're not really bothered about that. We just want to enjoy ourselves. Thank you all the same.'

I marvelled at his coolness. He hadn't even taken his eyes off the road. Now that was a class act.

'Fair enough,' said Pete. Then the van moved off.

'Good on you, Pedro,' laughed Jamie. 'That's put him off the scent.'

'Did you see who was with him?' asked Leo.

'I know,' said Carla. 'The fellow who put us out of the castle.'

'Same fellow who was talking to him last night in the pub,' went on Leo.

We cycled on in silence until we came to the top of a hill. Below us there was a wide lake to the right. On the left was a high hill, thick with trees.

'That's it!' exclaimed Jamie. 'That's Lough Hyne. We're there.'

'And so is someone else,' observed Carla.

Sure enough, parked at the junction of two roads was Pete's van.

'There's something I don't like about this,' said Pedro, dismounting. 'I get the feeling we're being followed. He's waiting to see which direction we'll take.'

'You could be right,' agreed Jamie. 'What can we do about it?'

'We should split up,' said Pedro. 'I feel responsible. After all it is Carla and I who got you three involved. I don't want to put you in any danger. I suggest that Carla and I take it from here.'

'And do what?' scoffed Jamie. 'Don't be daft. We're all in this together.'

'Pedro has a point, though,' I said.

'What do you mean?' Pedro asked, looking at me with those melted toffee eyes.

'About splitting up,' I went on. 'If we split into two groups, he wouldn't know which to follow.'

'Cripes, you're dead right, Maeve,' enthused Jamie. 'It might just work.'

'Indeed,' said Pedro. 'Jamie, if you and I acted as decoy, the other three could set up the inflatable. We could lose Pete and double back here. We'll just assume he doesn't realise that the island is the place we're looking for.'

'Why you and Jamie?' asked Leo peevishly. 'What about me?'

'Well,' said Pedro patiently. 'I'm the oldest here and he knows that I'm the person who's looking for the heirloom. I'm the one he'll be watching.'

'But why can't I come with you and Jamie?' persisted Leo.

'Because we girls will need a strong man to help us get the inflatable ready,' smiled Carla charmingly.

What kind of talk was this? Were we on some turn-of-the-century male macho trip? Jamie and Pedro heading the crooks off at the pass while we little misses batted our curly eyelashes and hid behind a little prat like Leo?

'Hold on there,' I said. 'What makes you think he'll follow you two and not us? What's so special about you two?'

Jamie and Pedro exchanged what is laughingly called a meaningful glance which made me seethe even more.

'Think about it, Maeve,' said Pedro. 'He knows I'm searching for whatever my ancestor has hidden.'

'But so is Carla,' I protested.

Pedro nodded patiently. 'Yes. But if you and Carla and Leo pretend to sit it out here, sunbathing, paddling or something harmless like that, Jamie and I will set off purposefully, making Pete think we're continuing our search.'

That sounded hairy and idiotic to me, but I agreed anyway.

'What about the inflatable?' asked Jamie. 'Can you girls...?'

'I can,' said Carla. 'I know how to set it up and attach the outboard motor. We have one of these at home.'

Pedro and Carla switched bikes so that she was pulling

the trailer. 'With any luck he'll think this is just picnic stuff,' said Pedro. 'And I'll be faster on your bike.'

'And what if he stops you?' I asked.

Jamie shook his head. 'He won't,' he said with determination. 'And even if he does stop us, what can he do?' He took a deep breath and glanced down to where the fish van was still parked.

'Just think,' he laughed nervously. 'What a bunch of fools we'll feel if Pete has a genuine reason to be there and that he has nothing whatever in his mind about the treasure.'

'We wish,' muttered Leo.

'Leo's right,' put in Pedro. 'There have been too many coincidences. Is everyone ready?'

We nodded. 'Right,' he continued. 'Be ready for us when we get back. Then we'll get across to the island and start our search in earnest. Be sure to hide your bikes well when he follows Jamie and me, as we hope he will.'

'Why?' asked Leo. 'Why hide the bikes?'

'Because,' said Jamie. 'If he comes back here we'll want him to think you've gone.'

'Let's hope it all goes according to plan,' said Carla. Then she lapsed into Spanish, to which Pedro responded with a string of what sounded like orders. I figured Spanish to be a bossy sort of language. My kind of language. I decided there and then to opt for it in school next year. Especially if I was going to be visiting Spain quite a lot.

We mounted up and free-wheeled down the hill. This might be much ado about nothing or it might be putting our heads in a noose. Whichever, there was no turning back now.

15

The Island

The two men in the van looked up as we sailed past. We made great play of giving them a cheery wave. We headed for a small marina where some dinghys were moored. This would be an ideal spot to set up our decoy plan. We parked our bikes and sat swinging our legs over the water, all the time keeping an eye on the van. Sure enough, the doors opened and the two figures emerged.

'The bait's been taken,' muttered Jamie. 'Time for us to get going, Pedro.'

The two boys grabbed their bikes and set off down the road. Carla, Leo and I lay back as if settling into a long sunbathing session (perish the thought, my legs screamed). The men hesitated, muttered for a moment and then hurried back to the van. We smothered our laughter as it swept past us.

'What a pair of nerds,' giggled Leo. 'They fell for it.'

We waited until the sound of the engine faded away. How they hoped to stay undetected behind the boys I don't know, but they were mighty anxious not to let them out of their sight.

'Quickly,' said Carla, undoing the string that held the inflatable in the trailer. She expertly manipulated something and, before you could say 'seasick', the thing swelled out into a sizeable rubber dinghy. With equal skill she attached the outboard motor.

'Ready,' she said, getting on board.

'Aren't we supposed to wait until the boys get back?' I asked. The thoughts of just a layer of rubber between me

115

and all that moving water gave me a few delirious moments.

Carla shook her head. 'Let's not chance it,' she said. 'Let's get on with the search. Time is against us. Hide the bikes while I get this going.'

Leo looked at me and I shrugged.

'Okay,' I said. 'You know best.' As far as I was concerned, when it came to matters nautical, anyone else knew best. We put the bikes deep into some bushes and ran back to the bobbing boat.

'Hang on,' called Carla above the noise. I gulped and concentrated on the island which was just a short distance away. If there was a ruined castle there, it was well hidden. Now and then my breakfast made valiant attempts at resurfacing, but within minutes Carla was guiding the boat through some rushes. Lithe as a sprite she hopped out into the shallow water and tied it to a tree-trunk. Leo and I leapt ashore after her.

'It's just a pile of old stones,' said Leo with disappointment in his voice.

'And what did you expect?' I asked. 'The whole clan O'Driscoll as a welcoming party and Labhras with the donkey ears waiting to serve us tea and sticky buns?'

Carla was ahead of us, anxiously searching the ground. 'Remember we are looking for a stone with a harp carved on it,' she said. 'Perhaps we should spread out.'

I wandered around, kicking at clumps of grass and turning over stones. I uncovered enough nasty crawlies to populate my nightmares for years to come. *What am I doing here?* I thought. *Stuck on a scrap of land in the middle of a lot of water, looking at stones in the company of nerdy Leo and a Spanish girl who just might steal Jamie. Not to mention Jamie and Pedro being chased by a loony in a van with lobsters painted on it.*

Just when I thought I was meeting the same stones over again, there was a cry of triumph from Leo.

'Look here!' he shouted.

He was standing by a heap of stones, the remains of an outer wall of the castle. One large stone stood apart from the others. It was to this stone that Leo was pointing. He looked at us with a mixture of delight and disbelief. 'Amn't I right?' he asked. 'Isn't that a harp?'

Carla and I bent down and examined the small, crude carving that was half covered by moss and weeds. 'Hard to say,' I muttered as Carla and I scraped them away. In

the time it takes to break several fingernails, we uncovered the whole carving. There was no doubt about it, this
was indeed a carving of a harp. Carla stood up and wiped
her hands on her shorts.

'I can't believe it,' she said. 'After all this time. The
barber's harp...'

'Don't get excited yet, Carla,' I put in. 'We still have to
find out if there's anything under it.'

The three of us heaved it out of the ground with much
gasping and panting. We stared at the dent left behind,
almost afraid to do anything else in case we'd be sorely
disappointed.

'Come on,' I said eventually. 'Let's get stuck in.'

We searched around for flattish stones and used them
as digging tools, taking turns at working the small area. It
was hot work. I could feel the damp sweat on my back
making my tee-shirt soggy. But we were so engrossed we
didn't feel the pain. Well, not much. I leaned back and
stretched my sweaty, but still elegant, neck and nodded
to Leo to take over. He tore into the task with his usual
enthusiasm, muck and grass flying everywhere. I was just
about to tell him to take it easy when he gave a whoop.

'I've hit something!' he cried. Sure enough a rectangular shape was beginning to form through the brown soil.
With our hands we brushed away the remaining soil and
uncovered a shape wrapped in coarse sacking. Carla carefully pushed aside the sacking and revealed a decorated
leather satchel with ornamental clasps.

'That's it,' whispered Carla. 'Can you believe it? This
is just so...'

'What is it?' I interrupted her awestruck wanderings.
'Aren't you going to open it?'

Very gingerly she lifted the satchel from where it had

lain all these years.

'Imagine,' I said. 'The last person who handled this was a dead guy hundreds of years ago.'

'He wasn't dead when he buried it, Maeve,' scoffed Leo.

Still, I had no desire to touch the thing. Carla was still staring at it disbelievingly. 'Go on,' I prompted her. 'See what's inside...' I broke off as Leo grabbed my arm.

'Ssshhh,' he was saying. 'Listen.'

We froze as the phut-phut of an engine being started reached us across the water. Carla gathered up the satchel and wrapped it again in the coarse sacking. We peered through the long grass towards the small marina. A boat with two figures in it was pointing this way. There was no mistaking that woolly hat.

'They came back!' I gasped. 'They're on to us.'

'Quickly,' said Carla. 'Back to the boat.'

We dashed the rest of the way and leapt aboard. Carla thrust the bundle into my hands while she got the engine going.

'Hurry up,' urged Leo. 'They've seen us.'

With a sudden burst, the engine sprang to life and we headed out across the lake.

16

A Dash Through the Rapids

'Where are you going?' I shouted to Carla over the noise of the engine. She was steering the inflatable towards a narrow channel between two high, rocky masses through which sea water entered the lake. Out there, I gulped at the thought, out there was the very large and wet ocean.

'There's no place else to go,' she replied. 'The lake is too small. They'd catch us in no time.'

I bit my lip, clutched the dead guy's satchel and prayed that I wouldn't be meeting him shortly. It flashed across my mind that Carla handled the boat very expertly for a girl who'd said that she and the sea were not good friends, but I didn't have time to think about that now.

'Rapids!' shouted Leo, who had propped himself up at the front like one of those figures you see stuck on the front of old-fashioned ships. As we neared the narrow channel, I could hear the roar of the gushing water over the sound of the engine. My parents would go ballistic, I thought, if they could see Leo and me charging through the churning sea with neither an adult nor life-jackets to save our necks.

'Hang on,' yelled Carla as she steered into the angry, white-foamed current which was cascading through the narrow opening. My breath was whipped away as we hit the first onslaught. All of a sudden the boat was being tossed about like one of those seriously tempestuous rides in Funderland. Only there was no gum-chewing guy to press a button and make it stop; this was the real thing.

All my parents' dire warnings exploded in my mind

with each dip and surge of the fragile little craft. With one hand I held on to a grip-rope attached to the side of the boat, with the other I hugged the mouldy bundle. Even in my hour of agony and probable death, I noted that it didn't feel like gold sovereigns. Could it be that we were risking our lives for old Don Pedro's laundry? As we swung backwards and forwards through the fuming waves, I caught odd glimpses of our pursuers. They were heading this way. The fools, could they not see what was ahead of them?

Leo was lying outstretched at the top of the inflatable, clutching the grip-rope. He grinned at me through the splashes and gave me a thumbs-up sign.

'Leo, hang on!' I shouted. If I survived this I didn't want to have him on my conscience if he were swept out to sea. Anyway, there are times when I feel really protective towards the little twerp. 'Don't let go!'

'What do you take me for?' he yelled back with more than a touch of scorn. 'Of course I'm holding on.'

Carla battled on. It amazed me that one so small and slight could keep up such a fight against the angry sea. Up in the air we seemed to fly, then down with a heavy bump into the roaring spume. They say your life flashes before you at times like this, but I must confess that whatever went before didn't matter a jot to me. It was the here and now that was overloading my conscious moments. Up again we sailed. I closed my eyes as down we plummeted, holding my breath against the next vicious rise. It didn't come. I opened my eyes. A very wet Carla looked at me with triumph.

'We did it!' she cried. 'We're through the rapids.'

I felt like jumping for joy. We were in normal water. Normal sea-water that stretched with choppy monotony to the horizon. I tried to focus on the fact that nothing could be worse than what we'd been through and held on to that thought.

'Keep going, Carla,' called Leo. 'Those two will get through if we did.'

Carla sprang into action again, keeping the boat on a steady course along the coastline. I was still clutching the leather satchel. The wrapping had got pretty wet, but at least everything was still in one piece and nothing had dropped out .

'Carla!' Leo shouted suddenly from his vantage point. 'There's a cave ahead. We could hide out there. They'll think we've gone around the bay. What do you say?'

She nodded and headed towards where Leo was pointing. Sure enough, tucked between the craggy rocks was a small cave. 'It will do until we get our breath back,' she said.

'Those rocks look mighty sharp,' I said. 'Do you think this heap of rubber will hold out? Does it carry its own puncture-repair outfit?'

Carla laughed. 'If it held out against the rapids, it will hold out against anything,' she said.

However, there wasn't much time for laughter. With Leo urging her on and guiding her between the scary rocks, she managed to manoeuvre the small craft into the cave. Here the water was calm and we could hopefully relax before the next crisis. Carla switched off the engine. The sudden silence gave the place an eerie atmosphere.

'I hope they don't cop on that we've come in here,' said Leo, voicing my own fears.

'It was the only thing we could do,' sighed Carla. 'I couldn't have gone any further. My arms are like lead.' She turned towards me. 'Thanks for keeping that safe.'

She nodded towards the bundle that I was still clutching.

Leo slid back along the boat. 'Let's see,' he said with his childish curiosity. 'What do you think it might be?'

I handed the satchel to Carla. It was hers after all. Besides I felt I'd embraced Don Pedro quite long enough, thank you.

Carla glanced towards the entrance of the cave. 'Sshhh,' she said, easing the boat closer to the side of the cave. With our hearts pounding we heard the approaching engine. Carla's knuckles were white as she gripped the satchel. We stared in disbelief as the boat carrying the two men passed the entrance to the cave. We didn't speak until we heard the engine fade away.

'Whew, they've gone,' said Leo with a great sigh of relief.

'Perhaps,' said Carla. 'They may come back.'

'Open the parcel,' said Leo. 'Give us a quick glance.'

Hardly daring to breathe, Carla eased the buckle of the satchel and opened it. She drew out a rectangular shape wrapped in more coarse cloth. I hoped it wouldn't turn out to be a mummified hand or something freaky like that. Carefully she unwrapped it. We gasped at what was uncovered.

'A BOOK!' I cried. 'All these death-defying stunts for a cruddy book! I don't believe this. What sort of an ancestor thinks of leaving his loved ones a ...' I was struck speechless.

'It's an old manuscript, like the Book of Kells,' said Leo, leaning closer to it. 'And look at the cover. It's got jewels stuck into it.'

'Look more like bits of coloured glass to me,' I snorted. 'Jewels are supposed to shine aren't they?'

'Maeve, it's been buried for a few hundred years,' said

Leo. 'What do you expect?'

'I was expecting some gold sovereigns or something jingly and valuable actually,' I retorted.

Carla said nothing. She was smiling as she ran her hands over the cover. 'We have it,' she said reverently. 'We actually have it, after all these years.'

'What do you mean "it"?' I asked. 'Did you know it was a stupid book?'

'No, no,' she laughed. 'Of course not. I just knew I'd be thrilled with whatever it turned out to be. And I am. It doesn't matter what it is, it is Don Pedro's gift to us, his descendants.'

'If I thought you knew all along that we were putting our heads in a noose for the sake of a tatty old book, I'd strangle you myself,' I said.

'Give over, Maeve,' put in Leo. 'Listen, those fellows might be back, shouldn't we get a move on?'

Carla nodded. 'You're right,' she sighed. There was a doubt in her voice. 'But if they come back and chase us, I don't think we'd have a chance.'

'Look,' I said, ever one to come to the rescue. 'There are loads of high ledges up there. Why don't we hide it on one of them. Then, if they do catch up with us, we'll have nothing.'

'Good idea,' said Leo. 'Then we can come back with Jamie and Pedro and get it back. That makes sense, Carla.'

Carla thought it over for a moment. Then she smiled. 'It makes very good sense,' she said. 'Let's do that.'

We edged the boat over until it was right up against some flattish rocks. I jumped out and reached out for the book. Carla hesitated, as if having second thoughts. Then she put it back into the leather satchel, wrapped the sacking around it once more and handed it to me.

'We'll just ease up to the entrance to see if there is any sign of the two men,' she said. 'If they come back while you're still up there...'

'Then you two head off and I'll stay hidden until you can get back for me.' I couldn't believe I was saying this. Did I really mean that I'd stay stuck up on a ledge in a damp cave minding a book that nobody could read? I marvelled at how easy it is to get carried away with the drama and emotion of a time like this.

'Oh, Maeve, you're simply wonderful,' said Carla.

Then again, I mused, her brother would be sure to say

the same thing and that was reason enough to throw my natural common sense out of the window. I climbed quite easily on to a high ledge which ran almost the length of one side of the cave. There were many bits of rock sticking up, forming natural little niches. I carefully avoided the small slabs of loose slate that littered the ledge.

As Carla and Leo were now posted near the entrance to the cave, I opened the satchel and eased out the book again, just to see if there was anything I was missing out on. There was enough light coming in for me to see quite well. I flicked through the pages. They were all in Latin. I knew this because we'd done a bit of Latin in first year so there were enough words for me to recognise. Except for the bit inside the cover. Both the lettering and the language here were different. When I got used to the curly bits and the weird creatures twisted into painful contortions, I realised that this bit was in Irish. Again I recognised some of the words, but before I could make sense of them, Carla and Leo were heading back. Then I put the book back and pushed the bundle into a dry niche higher up.

'Okay?' asked Carla.

I nodded and clambered down from the ledge. 'It's safe as houses,' I said as I caught Leo's outstretched hand and dropped into the boat.

'Are you ready to hang on again?' asked Carla.

'What do you mean?' I asked.

'We have to go back the way we came,' she said. 'Those two will be looking out for us if we continue around the bay. The only way back is through the lake and across to our bikes.'

'The rapids,' I said, like a zombie. *Please could I be unconscious for the next half-hour or so?*

'It won't be so bad,' said Carla. 'We were against the tide when we were coming out. We'll be with it going through this time. It will carry us with it.'

'It will be all right, Maeve,' said Leo, squeezing my arm. 'You'll see. We'll be fine.'

My first thought was to get back on the ledge and sit out however long it would take to get something solid and safe like the lifeboat and its crew of large, capable men to rescue me. But I figured it might be better to get this over and done with. I prepared myself for my second death that day.

17

Trouble for Carla and Pedro?

Compared to the last battle with the rapids, the return journey wasn't quite so bad. That doesn't mean that it was a doddle. Oh, no. Once more we were tossed about like fleas in a jacuzzi, but at least we knew we were being shoved in the right direction.

'Gushing water!' shouted Leo.

'What?'

'Gushing water. This must be what Don Pedro meant by gushing water. In his letter,' he added at our puzzled faces. Then it dawned on me. 'Of course!' I exclaimed. 'That's exactly what it is. He must have either come in or gone out through the narrow channel.'

'He was certainly right about the gushing,' said Carla. 'I don't think my arms will ever recover.'

'You poor thing,' I sympathised. 'You were terrific, though, the way you handled the boat. You must be very experienced at this lark.'

Carla shrugged. 'I've done a bit of sailing,' she said dismissively. 'I don't much like it, but I'll do it when I have to. Look,' she went on, pointing to the marina.

'It's Jamie and Pedro!' exclaimed Leo. He stood up and began waving like mad.

'Sit down, Leo,' I cried. 'You're rocking the boat.'

Both Carla and Leo looked at me in amazement and burst out laughing. At first I couldn't understand their callous response to my plea, but then I saw the reason for their mirth. I'd just survived the most tempestuous hurtling about in the boat and here I was getting jittery

128

about a little bit of rocking on calm water. I grinned sheepishly.

We could see that Pedro's face was looking a bit on the thundery side as we drew towards the shore. Even in anger his face was one to die for. But then, of course, I'd nearly done just that.

'Where have you been?' he said. 'The plan was that you'd wait until we doubled back...'

'We got it!' shouted Leo. 'We found it!'

'What?' Jamie and Pedro cried out together.

'He's right,' said Carla, reaching out for the boys' outstretched hands to pull us ashore. 'We really found it.'

'You've actually found the book!' Pedro still couldn't believe it. He looked into the boat. 'Where is it?'

'We've hidden it,' I said. 'Pete and his side-kick chased us, so we hid in a cave and put it on a high ledge in case they came back after us. We can get it later.'

In his excitement Pedro lapsed into Spanish again.

Leo was glancing anxiously towards the rapids. 'No sign of them,' he said. 'But they'll surely be back. I bet they'll cop on that we came back through the rapids.'

Jamie's jaw dropped. 'You never...' he began. 'And with no life-jackets!'

I felt my smile spread with glorious triumph from ear to ear. 'We certainly did,' I said. 'Both ways.'

'It was mega,' laughed Leo. 'We were nearly killed dozens of times. You missed it, Jamie.'

Jamie looked at me in amazement. 'It's true,' I said. 'Every word. Look, we're still soaking wet.'

'But Maeve,' said Jamie. 'You in a boat ...'

'Ah,' I laughed. 'Me in a boat and not throwing up! Me in a boat in death-defying circumstances and surviving without a hiccup. Is that thought giving you a problem?'

Jamie was shaking his head, awestruck. 'That channel is notorious,' he said. 'The incoming tide gushes through it on the way in and on the way out. It's mentioned on Dad's charts. And you did it in an inflatable!'

'It was nothing,' I laughed.

Nothing! I'd have shaved my head rather than set foot in that rubber dinghy if I'd known what was ahead.

'We'd better pack the inflatable and get out of here,' Pedro was saying. 'If we leave it moored here it could get sabotaged by those two crooks. No point in going back now while they're still on the prowl. We'll come back when we know it's safe to do so. You're sure the book is well hidden?' he said, looking at me.

'Absolutely,' I replied. 'Even if it occurs to them to go into the cave there's no way they'd find it. Only Carla or Leo or me can do that.'

'Okay,' said Pedro, pressing the deflated boat into the trailer. 'So long as you are sure. We'll watch out for the two men and, as soon as we're sure they're ensconced in the pub or something, we'll go back and retrieve the book. Okay?'

'Okay,' we all agreed. I tried not to dwell on the fact that we'd have to go through those rapids again, but, hey, we were getting good at cheating the Grim Reaper by now. And at least we'd have Jamie and Pedro with us next time.

On the way back we told Jamie and Pedro about our find and the chase.

'You actually went through those rapids?' now it was Pedro's turn to be gobsmacked.

'Gushing water,' I said. 'That's the gushing water mentioned in the letter. Don Pedro's been there and done that.'

'I said that,' put in Leo, peeved at me for stealing his thunder. 'I thought of that.' Who cared?

'I still can't believe it,' said Pedro when we'd finished our excited telling and retelling of our tale. Everyone was in high spirits as we free-wheeled down the last hill towards Baltimore. Everyone except me.

I was having trouble with my brain. Some people, like Jamie and – I have to admit it – Leo, have the kind of brains that slot events into neat categories which can sort out the delights from the dregs. My particular brain is a bit like a mixing bowl; everything gets tossed in and stirred up together. The result was that, although I knew I should be outrageously happy after today's goings-on, something was gnawing at my mind.

Was it the thoughts of being tossed through those rapids again? That had to be it. That was the only thing I could think of that was cutting across the bliss of being a heroine.

'You're strangely quiet, Maeve,' said Jamie, cycling beside me. 'Are you all right?'

'Me?' I forced a laugh. 'I'm fine. I'm just so thrilled about all of this. Who'd have thought we'd actually find old Don Pedro's silly book.'

The book! Was that it? Something about the book. I tried to get my thoughts to make some sense. Was I disappointed it was only a book? Nag, nag – but whatever was bugging my brain just wouldn't make itself known.

'Pity it's only a book,' I said aloud, just to see if saying it would banish the bug. 'I was expecting something better. Gold, maybe. Or some glitzy jewels.'

'What are you saying?' asked Jamie. 'If it's something along the lines of the Book of Kells, it's a priceless piece of work. Better than gold.'

'Maybe I'm just tired,' I said. 'Tired and wet.'

'Who's tired?' asked Pedro, turning his head towards us. 'Maeve?'

'Just a bit,' I said. 'I'll be fine after a hot shower and a triple-decker sandwich.'

'You do that,' said Pedro. 'Relax, you've been wonderful.'

We were now at the lane leading to Jamie's place.

'Aren't you coming in?' he asked, as Carla and Pedro made to move on.

'I want to change my clothes,' said Carla. 'And my hair is so full of salt water I must wash it. I need to get some shampoo from the village.'

I was about to tell her that she could have some of Lady Codology's frightfully expensive stuff, but that might be overstepping Jamie's hospitality. And his patience.

'We'll be up later,' said Pedro, giving me one of those brilliant smiles that zapped my troublesome brain bug. 'We'll celebrate.'

After my shower and a fairly disastrous sandwich (fish fingers, bananas, crisps, raw mushrooms and peanut butter do not relate well between two slices of bread), I stretched out in the sun on a window-seat and promptly fell asleep.

My dreams really stirred things up in that mixing bowl of a brain. Fragmented words and phrases in Irish, words that had stuck in my mind from the book I'd hidden – like *ón áthair go dtí an mac is sine* and *áirneís luachmhar teaghlaigh* and *bíodh sé mar sin* – were mixed up with dancing flamingos, a barber's harp and stormy seas. I was more exhausted when I woke up than I'd been before I fell asleep.

What woke me was a rhythmic clang of something being struck. Leo was out on the patio flicking stones at a row of old Coke cans. I looked at my watch and was amazed to see that I'd been asleep for an hour and a half. Boy, I thought, near-death experiences really make you tired. I rapped at the window.

'Where's Jamie?' I asked.

'He nipped down to the village to get some milk,' he said. 'Oh, here he is.'

Sure enough Jamie was cycling up the lane. He seemed to be in a great hurry. Cripes, we weren't that desperate for milk. He tossed his bike against the bushes, shouted to Leo and barged into the house.

'I saw Pete's van in the village,' he panted. 'No sign of him, but I didn't hang about to see. We've got to move. Come on, down to the hostel quickly, and get Carla and Pedro.'

Leo and I didn't need a second prompting. Within moments the three of us were off. The evening sun flashed between the gaps in trees and bushes, making the ride seem like some weird strobe-disco-on-wheels. We were so anxious to get to Carla and Pedro that none of us spoke. Talk would have been a waste of valuable time. We dismounted in the cobbled courtyard of the hostel and I held Jamie's bike while he ran to Carla and Pedro's chalet. He tried the door. It was locked. He peered through the window and looked back at Leo and me with a puzzled expression.

'No sign of them,' he said.

'Ask the man in charge,' suggested Leo.

As Jamie ran towards the main building, Leo turned to me. 'Where do you think they might be?' he asked. 'Do you think...do you think Pete and his band might have taken them away?' he gulped. 'They could be forcing Carla and Pedro to tell them where the book is.'

'Don't be daft,' I said. But I had an uneasy feeling. That stupid book. It was causing more problems than it was worth. Those Irish phrases and words that had dogged my dreams now came rushing back into my head. I knew some of them were words I should understand, if I had the time to think about them. But this was not the time. Jamie was coming back.

'They've gone,' he said.

'What do you mean "gone"?' I asked.

He looked at me with a mixture of anger and anxiety. 'How gone do they have to be?' he said. 'They've simply gone, vamoosed, checked out of the hostel.'

'Both of them?' I asked.

Jamie shook his head. 'The manager only saw Pedro. He paid the bill about half an hour ago. The manager said he seemed to be in a terrible hurry. He helped him to load up his bike. Carla's bike was still outside the chalet, but when the manager asked if she'd be back for it, Pedro got very agitated. He just muttered something in Spanish and cycled off. But here's the worst bit...' Jamie paused.

'What? For heaven's sake, Jamie,' I snapped.

Jamie swallowed. 'The manager's wife said she saw Carla about an hour earlier in the village. She was with an older man.'

'I knew it!' cried Leo. 'Pete!'

I bit my lip. This wasn't sounding at all good.

Jamie was nodding. 'He must have taken Carla,' he said. 'Probably waited until Pedro was over at the showers or something and forced Carla away.'

'Shampoo!' I exclaimed.

'What?'

'She said she had to get some shampoo in the village. Pete must have nabbed her then!'

'Does that mean he's holding her as a hostage?' asked Leo. I was almost afraid to hear the answer.

'Looks that way,' said Jamie. 'He and his mate must have gone around the bay and got back before us. They probably waited their chance to snatch either Carla or Pedro...'

'And, when they got Carla, they made Pedro check out of here and meet them somewhere to take them to the place where the treasure is,' I put in.

'And what will they do with when they get the book?' asked Leo. 'Why make them check out?'

'They'll more than likely take them away by boat and leave them stranded ashore somewhere miles up the coast,' said Jamie. 'Far enough away to enable Pete's lot to get away. They must have made them check out so that there would be no questions asked here. Made it look like Carla and Pedro were just moving on.'

'But wouldn't Pedro have told the manager that his sister had been forced away?' asked Leo. 'Surely he'd get him to ring the guards.'

Jamie was shaking his head again. 'Think about it,' he said. 'They probably told Pedro that Carla would be harmed if he tried to get help. What would you do in a case like that if it was your sister?'

Leo nodded miserably. 'The rotten prats,' he muttered.

'God, it doesn't bear thinking about,' I said. 'What will we do?'

Jamie's face suddenly came alive. 'We'll get there ahead of them!' he said. 'We'll get the book. When they find out it's gone, they'll have no choice but to let Carla and Pedro go.'

'Should we not tell the guards...?' I began.

'No time,' said Jamie. 'Come on, we'll have to be quick.' He jumped on to his bike and Leo and I followed him. Then he suddenly swung back towards the house.

'Where are you going?' I shouted.

'You'll see,' he called back. 'Hurry.'

This was not the time to be getting stuck into a debate about directions. Jamie must be pretty sure of his intentions, I thought. He's not about to do anything thick.

'I hope,' I said aloud as I pushed my sunburnt legs into action.

'Hope what?' asked Leo, puffing to keep up. But I'd gone ahead. All I could think of was that our friends were in trouble and that it was up to Jamie, Leo and me to get them out of it.

18

A Race Against Time

We followed Jamie as he charged up to the house. He threw down his bike and ran around to where the sailing stuff was kept. Leo and I still didn't know what he was at, but we trusted him.

'Grab a life-jacket each,' he said as we caught up with him. 'We'll be heading out into the open sea.'

My heart did a double somersault. Not more sailing. Please, not again. This time I would surely die.

'Move it, Maeve,' commanded Jamie. He was pulling the life-jackets from a shelf. He threw a sailing map to Leo. 'Look after that, Leo. Maeve, take that compass.'

I unselfishly and heroically pushed all thoughts of my own death to one side and did as I was told. The three of us ran down to the bay to where the dinghy was moored.

'What are you doing?' I said at last.

'We'll beat them to it,' said Jamie. 'They've probably gone by the lake. By the time they get there and make their way through the rapids, we'll have gone around the coast and got there before them.'

Within minutes he had the engine sparked into life and Leo and I leapt aboard. I tried not to think of that totally terrible sandwich I'd eaten earlier as we bobbed up and down. Instead I tried to concentrate on the fact that we were heading into the clutches of a band of crooks who'd stop at nothing to get their hands on Don Pedro's silly old book. Maybe the sandwich was a better thought.

'All this for an old book,' I said, as another wave lifted us up.

Jamie's eyes were fixed on the route ahead as he expertly guided the tiller. 'I've told you,' he said. 'It's a priceless manuscript.'

'You didn't even see it,' I retorted. 'It could be pages of junk for all you know.'

'No,' he agreed. 'But from what you say it sounds like a major find. Why would Don Pedro have gone to all that trouble to hide it if it wasn't valuable? If it was valuable then, it's hundreds of times more valuable now.'

'Who'd want it?' I went on.

'There are billionaires in places like Japan or Germany or America who'd pay a lot of money for an old artefact like that,' he replied. 'Just for the privilege of owning it.'

'No wonder those blokes are so desperate,' said Leo. 'I hope,' he turned back towards Jamie and me and swallowed hard, 'I hope Pedro and Carla will be all right.'

'If we can just get the book before those guys, they'll have no reason to hold Carla and Pedro,' said Jamie.

'Is it for Carla you're doing this?' The question had slipped out before I'd time to catch it and strangle it. You know how it is, a thought hits you and your mouth goes into overdrive.

Jamie looked at me in amazement. 'Maeve, is that all you can think...?'

'All right, all right,' I said. 'Forget I asked.' I stared straight ahead so that he wouldn't see my acute embarrassment. *Open up, waters, and swallow me*, I thought. Not that the waters needed any encouragement, they were making a jolly good attempt at doing just that.

We hugged the coastline as we rounded the hill where the beacon stood. I glanced up at it, shining white in the late sun, and marvelled at how much had happened since the time Carla and I had thrown our soggy sandwiches to the gulls. I thought of Carla's laughing face and I gritted my teeth; nobody was going to harm my friend. Nor her hunky brother.

'Come on,' I urged Jamie.

'This is as fast as it will go.' I had to be content with that.

'Look,' said Leo, pointing back the way we'd come. 'There goes your Brad Pitt, Maeve.'

Sure enough, the big yacht was starting to move this way.

'And I never even found out what celebrity has missed out on meeting me,' I said. 'Well, it's his loss. I'll mention this in my memoirs and he'll be dead sick he shunned my company.'

'It might have only been the old guy we glimpsed on our way to Sherkin,' said Jamie.

'No way,' I said. 'He's just the manservant who polishes the brass and makes Brad's cocoa.'

The bit of light-hearted banter took our minds off the pending danger for a few moments. We fell silent as we rounded the bay and were confronted by the open sea. With one eye on the map and the other on the coastline, Jamie guided us like a true navigator. This was the guy I'd called a prat and a wimp? He caught me looking at him and he grinned. I brushed imaginary dust from my shorts and pretended to be examining my legs. They were turning a nice shade of brown. Rather, the bits that weren't peeling off like old tissues were turning brown. The overall effect was an interesting shade of piebald, but at least the soreness had subsided somewhat.

'There it is!' shouted Leo. 'Just ahead. I recognise the bit of rock that's sticking out. I remember wondering if it would puncture the inflatable.'

Jamie lowered the noise of the engine and we almost free-wheeled – or whatever it is that boats do when they're not propelled – up to the cave. We listened, with pounding hearts, but all we could hear was the swish of the water as it washed into the cave.

'I think we're in luck,' said Jamie. 'I think we've managed to get here before them.' He revved the engine again and we sailed into the cave. Leo and I guided him over to the ledge where I'd been only hours before. I leapt out on to the rocks and climbed up to the ledge. Sure enough, there was the sacking-wrapped bundle safe and sound.

'Hey!' shouted Leo, looking towards the entrance to the cave. 'That big yacht.'

'What about it?' I asked, reaching out for the bundle.

'It seems to have moored out there,' said Leo. 'That's strange.'

'Never mind that,' said Jamie. 'Grab the book, Maeve, and let's get out of here.'

Before I could move there was the sound of an engine as into the cave sailed Pete and his side-kick. We all froze. It was I who found voice first.

'What have you done with them?' I asked angrily from my perch. 'Where are Carla and Pedro?'

'What are you talking about, girl?' asked Pete. 'Will you just listen to me about what you have hidden, please? It's of great value...'

'I know that,' I retorted. 'I know what you're after, Pete. But this doesn't belong to you. It belongs to Carla and Pedro.'

'Let them go,' put in Jamie. 'There's no point in holding them. You can't take away what belongs to them. Tell us where they are and we'll say no more about this.'

'Prats!' shouted Leo. 'Lay off Carla and Pedro.'

The two men looked at one another. 'I don't know what you're talking about,' said Pete. 'But...'

'Oh, no. Of course you don't,' scoffed Jamie. 'Pull the other one. You've been shadowing us since we first told you about the letter.'

The side-kick said nothing. He just shook his head.

I felt a sudden pang of guilt. I was responsible for Pete and company being here. 'Tell us where they are,' I growled with as much menace as I could muster.

They looked up at me. 'Listen...' began Pete.

He broke off as another engine sound approached. An inflatable sailed into the cave. This was getting to be quite a party. I couldn't believe it when I saw who was on board.

'Carla! Pedro!' I shouted gleefully. 'You're all right.' I recognised the inflatable as the one we'd been on earlier. They must have used it to get away from the two crooks, I thought.

'Whew! We thought you'd been kidnapped by these guys,' said Jamie.

Leo was jumping up and down dangerously in the boat. 'Oh, this is great,' he shouted. 'You're safe.'

Once more the mixer in my brain was stirring up into overdrive. This time it was to do with the inflatable.

'Maeve,' said Pedro. 'I'm so glad you've found Don Pedro's treasure. Will you pass it down to me? You've saved our father's vineyard. We'll be forever in your debt, the three of you.'

'You're brill, Maeve,' went on Carla. 'A true friend.'

Pete began shouting at the occupants of Pedro's boat. I reached again for the sacking-wrapped satchel and tried to make sense of the situation. There had to be some way to sort all this out, to get the book safely to Carla and Pedro. *Think, Maeve,* I told myself. *Think quickly.*

Jamie and Leo seemed to be dumbstruck as the barrage of words went back and forth from boat to boat.

'Our ancestor...' began Carla.

'Your ancestor was a thief who stole this book from the O'Driscoll chieftain who sheltered him,' said Pete. 'The story of this book has been handed down from generation to generation throughout the centuries. This book belongs...'

'Rubbish!' shouted Pedro. 'You're talking rubbish. Maeve,' he looked up at me with his melted toffee eyes, 'after all we've been through together, let me have the book now.'

The second man in Pete's boat stood up.

'No!' he cried. He had such an authoritative voice that everyone stopped. '"This precious book of prayer was presented by the monks of the Abbey of Saint Baire to Fionn Mor O'Driscoll in gratitude for his protection and succour during troubled times..."' he broke off quoting when Pedro shouted him down in excited Spanish.

The mind-mixer in my head was slowing down. Things were falling into place.

'Go on,' I shouted to the man who had been speaking. 'Finish what you were quoting.'

Everyone looked up at me with dismay, but I only had eyes and ears for the man. He turned towards me. '"This sacred book will pass from father to oldest son and from him to his oldest son from generation to generation and it shall thus remain as a precious heirloom for all time. Let it be so..."' Again Petro interrupted.

'Come on, Maeve,' he called up to me. 'Give me the book you've helped us to find. My father will...'

'No, wait!' I cried. My stumbling Irish was beginning to make sense. For an old wrinkly our Irish teacher was pretty cool. He livened up the boring grammar bits by telling us stories and legends which made the language come alive for us. Now this was beginning to pay off; the words that the man was quoting fitted in with the Irish inscription – the words that had been haunting my dreams. *'Ón áthair go dtí an mac is sine'* – from father to oldest son, *'áirneís luachmhar teaghlaigh'* – precious family heirloom, *'bíodh sé mar sin'* – let it be so.

'Maeve, give me the book,' Pedro was beginning to sound angry. His eyes were no longer like melted toffee, more like brittle nut-crunch – hard and glittering.

I began to come down from the ledge, stopping half way. 'I don't think so, Pedro,' I said, as evenly as my nervousness would let me. 'I don't think this is yours.'

I was only barely conscious of Jamie's startled cry and Leo's gobsmacked face.

'Don't be silly, Maeve,' said Carla. 'You've heard my story. You know it belongs to us.'

Pedro reached into a pocket of the boat and produced something that made me gasp.

'A gun!' shouted a shocked Leo. Everyone froze.

'Right,' Pedro said. 'Now, Maeve, hand over the book.'

To think that I'd risked my elegant neck in a rubber boat and that I'd sweated over writing award-winning poetry for this – this swine who was pointing a GUN at me. I was very cross indeed. True love disintegrated like a meringue in muck.

'What I'm going to do, you cheating liar,' I said, 'is this. I'm going to throw this stupid book into the water. If you think you can pick up thieving from where your miserable old failure of a tin-hatted ancestor left off, then

think again. It will sink like his leaky tub of a Spanish ship.' I raised the sacking over my head.

'Don't!' shouted Pete. 'Don't do that, girl. Let them have it. Let them take it away. It is a thing of great beauty. Please let them have it rather than destroy it.'

While he was speaking, Jamie had dashed off the boat and clambered up to stand in front of me. 'Go on, then,' he shouted to Pedro. 'Shoot your gun, Pedro.'

Jamie! My Jamie was protecting me! Just like in the movies. This was heavy macho stuff. Pedro was taken aback, but only for a moment. He raised the gun. Now it was my turn.

'Take it, Pedro,' I cried. Then I tossed the sacking-wrapped parcel towards the deepest water in the cave. Everyone watched in horrified silence as it settled for a few seconds on the water and then disappeared out of sight. All hell broke loose. Both Pedro and Carla spat strings of Spanish invective in my direction.

'Save your breath,' I said from my perch. 'I don't know what you're saying and I don't care. The book doesn't exist any more so buzz off – back to your yacht and the ould fella who's been skulking there. You're a pair of lying crooks.'

Jamie, still standing in front of me, joined in. 'Just go, both of you,' he said with dignity. 'You have no further business here.'

Still spewing insults, the pair of them gunned the engine and sped from the cave.

'That's your inflatable,' I whispered to Jamie as we watched them go.

'It doesn't matter. Just so long as they're gone.'

Now was the time to let my wobbly knees have their way. The adrenaline had stopped coursing through my body and I collapsed like a rag-doll on the rocks. In a flash Pete and his pal were up to help Jamie to get me down the rest of the way. But I pushed their hands away.

'Just give me a sec,' I said, taking a few deep breaths.

'You were very brave, girl,' said Pete. 'But you should have let them have the book. You needn't have done what you did. If only you knew ... Oh lord, girl, if only you'd waited...'

'They didn't deserve to have it,' said Jamie.

I looked up at Jamie. Jamie, my action-packed hero who'd put himself between me and a bullet 'You're the one who was brave,' I said.

'Me?' he laughed.

'You jumped in front of me. Or had you forgotten that you nearly had yourself killed for me? That freak was pointing a gun. Don't pretend to be so blasé. We could be scraping you off the wall right now.'

Jamie laughed again. 'Gun?' he said. 'That was no gun, Maeve. That was just a gadget for sending flares – distress signals. That wouldn't have done any harm. We'd have been well down behind the rocks before a flare would reach us.'

Well, there went that bit of romantic drama down the tubes. Still, he did climb up to be with me.

'Could we dive for it?' asked Leo from the boat. 'The book, could we dive for it?'

Pete shook his head. 'No point, lad. It's well destroyed by now,' he said.

'Was it really yours?' asked Jamie.

Pete nodded towards the other man. 'We're O'Driscolls, Tim and me,' he said. 'It was our branch of the family who hid Don Pedro from the English. He stole silver and gold from Fionn O'Driscoll and his family, but the thing that caused them the most heartbreak was the theft of the precious book that the monks had given to Fionn Mor. He'd protected them against the soldiers who were sent to sack the monasteries during the reign of Henry the Eighth.'

'The only thing that could be passed from father to oldest son,' put in Tim, 'was the inscription that had been learnt by heart.'

'For all those centuries?' said Jamie, sitting down beside me on the rocks. 'Your family have been saving that inscription for all those centuries?'

'For all those centuries,' said Tim. 'Generations have tried to find the book, but all we knew was that it had never left the country, that it was hidden somewhere within a short radius of Castletownshend.'

'That's where he was caught,' put in Pete.

'Don Pedro was caught?' I said.

Pete nodded. 'He still had some of the silver on him, but he would never tell where he'd buried the book.'

'All this time,' marvelled Jamie. 'To think that this story has been nursed in both families, one in Ireland and one in Spain, for all this time.'

'We're a proud people,' said Tim. 'Our heritage means a lot to us. The feeling of our family for this manuscript has been carried from generation to generation, even after our land was taken from us. And now...' He nodded sadly and looked at where I'd tossed the wretched thing into the water.

'You shouldn't have ordered us out of that castle like that,' I said to Tim. While sore points were up for airing, I might as well get mine in. 'You'd think we were going to trash the miserable dump the way you went on. If you're so protective why don't you clean it up?'

Tim smiled. 'No,' he agreed. 'I shouldn't have done that. But I suppose I felt I was protecting part of my ancestry. I thought you were a bunch of youngsters on...'

'On a cider binge or a drugs session,' said Jamie with more than a touch of scorn.

'Yes,' admitted Tim. 'Didn't give you a chance, did I? Sorry about that. It's just that we do sometimes get bunches of drop-outs hanging about there.'

A tad freaky, I thought, getting his knickers in a knot over an ancestral backyard. But this time I swallowed the remark before my mouth could utter it. 'And what about you?' I said to Pete. 'Why didn't you say something when we showed you the letter – you recognised it, didn't you? Why didn't you say so?'

It was Pete's turn to look scornful. 'Would you have said so if you were me?'

'You needn't have sent us off to Sherkin,' I added, thinking I might as well throw everything at these two extremely odd men who couldn't let go of their hairy past. 'That was more than a bit sneaky. I was struck down with sunstroke. I'll be scarred for life, thanks to you. My future as a top model is ruined due to your lies.'

'Yes,' shouted Leo. 'That was a rotten trick.'

Pete grimaced and shook his head. 'I'm sorry,' he said.

'You thought you'd get us out of the way while you tried to work out the translation?' put in Jamie. 'Send us on a wild-goose chase. You don't exactly come up smelling of roses, you two. If you'd taken the time to come clean, to tell us the truth...'

'How could I do that, lad?' exclaimed Pete. 'Sure you were in cahoots with those two Spaniards. Do you think they'd have let us tell the truth? What else could I do?'

Both sides were silenced into a sort of stalemate; both had done right and wrong with the best of intentions.

Pete sighed and said, 'Sorry. Too late now anyway, the book is lost forever, so nobody is the victor.'

'I'm sorry about your book,' muttered Jamie. 'If only we'd known.'

'You did what you thought was right,' said Pete with an air of resignation. He turned to me. 'Will you be all right?' he asked. 'Hold my arm and we'll get you back to your boat.'

'I'm okay,' I said, pulling myself up. 'I don't need your help. I just want to get out of this place.'

Pete nodded and made his way down to his boat. I watched him join his brother. Two elderly men who'd been carrying the pride of their ancestors all these years; there was something pathetic yet very proud about them. 'Tell me,' I said impulsively, what would you have done with the book? Jamie says it's worth an awful lot of money.'

'Money has nothing to do with it,' said Tim, as he prepared to push off his boat. 'It would have been put on display in the National Museum.'

'The pride of that would have been enough,' put in Pete. 'The O'Driscoll pride would be all the payment we'd ask. It was never a question of money with us.'

'Are you sure?' I asked. 'Would you swear on your family's graves that you'd no interest in the money?'

'Don't go on about it, Maeve,' whispered Jamie to me. 'You're going over the top. Let them go.'

Pete looked up at me as he prepared to cast off. 'It doesn't matter now,' he said. 'It's down there where it will never be of use to anyone. And yes, to answer your question, I'd swear in any court of law that money was never an issue in relation to that manuscript. That was something that went far beyond the value of money. You meant well by destroying it rather than letting those two get their hands on it, but it would have been better to let them have it. At least we could have gone through some legal procedures to try to get it back.'

'Will you children be all right?' asked Tim, just before turning on the engine. 'Do you want to keep up with us?'

'No need,' I said. 'We'll just rest for a minute.'

The two men nodded and turned their boat towards the sea. We watched until they'd disappeared.

'Well,' said Jamie, getting ready to follow, 'that was lively. It's all over now. All that fuss and excitement for ... for...' He looked down into the water.

'For nothing,' finished Leo. 'If only we'd known we could have saved the book.'

Now was the moment for my next piece of drama.

'We did!' I said.

'What?' they both yelled together, looking up at me.

'We *did* save it,' I went on. 'You must take me for a right eejit. Do you really think I'd toss that book away just like that?'

'What are you saying, Maeve?' said Jamie when he'd found his voice.

'I didn't throw the book into the water,' I said. 'When I saw the two boyos sail into the cave I switched the book for a flat stone that I wrapped in the sacking. I'd intended throwing that into the water to deceive them, but it served the same purpose to get rid of Pedro and Carla.'

Jamie and Leo were looking up at me with varying expressions of amazement and gobsmackery. Maeve the All-Powerful had struck again. I was getting to like this power thing.

'What are you saying, Maeve?' asked Jamie again.

I climbed back up to the ledge and produced the leather satchel. 'Here we are,' I said, easing out the book.'It's all here, complete with curly letters and po-faced saints. Here's the O'Driscoll manuscript.'

Jamie began to laugh. Leo and I joined in. Our laughter rang around the cave.

'Why didn't you give it to them?' asked Leo. 'Why didn't you let Pete and Tim have it?'

'Ha, I wouldn't hand it over just like that,' I said. 'We've already been had by people we trusted.' I looked at Jamie. 'Your parents are due back this evening. I want to talk to them about this. They'll know what to do.'

Jamie grinned. 'You're something else, Maeve Morris,' he said.

19

A Settling of Ancestral Dust

'Well, we'll look forward to seeing that manuscript in the Museum,' said Mr Stephenson as we drove back from Skibbereen. I thanked my stars that we'd discussed the whole messy business with Jamie's parents. As I'd figured, they knew exactly what to do. We'd been shunted around from coastguard to garda station to solicitor's office. Now everything was legally settled. The O'Driscolls had signed papers to reclaim their ancient book and signed some more to donate it to the state on behalf of their ancestors. Needless to say they'd been ecstatic. If I'd asked them for the moon they'd have flown up there in their lobster van and got it for me.

Mrs Stephenson was leaning with one arm on the front seat so that she was facing us. 'What a fantastic story,' she said. 'I still can't believe it. Maeve, you amaze me. You all amaze me.' She was looking with open pride at her son.

Of course she'd gone ballistic when we'd first confronted herself and Mr Stephenson with our hairy escapades and how Carla and Pedro had conned us into helping them.

'The wretches,' she had summed up. 'Deceiving you – deceiving all of us – like that. Weren't you foolish...' She'd broken off when she saw steam coming from my ears and nostrils. 'Foolish' was hardly the word to describe our eminently outstanding feats of courage. She'd then bared her expensive dental work and changed her tune. 'But very brave. You were all so brave. Especially you, Maeve.' There had been a slight catch in her voice. I wondered was she overcome with intense emotion or was she choking on uttering my name. Probably the latter, but who cared?

'Poor child' and 'Dear' had become history. Not saying that we were now bosom pals. Not likely, but we respected one another's territory. She accepted that I was Jamie's good friend and I'd accepted that she couldn't help being a control freak with a maternal guilt trip. Jamie had proved his point and I reckoned she'd bite back her attack on any further statements he'd make to establish his independence.

'That big yacht,' Leo was saying.

'What about it?' asked Mr Stephenson as he narrowly avoided a sleeper van that leapt at us around a bend in the road.

'To think that it was their boat all the time and they never even hinted,' went on Leo. 'They never let on it was their uncle who was moored out there.'

'So much for Brad Pitt,' laughed Jamie, grinning at me.

'Brad who?' asked Mrs Stephenson. Then, when she realised this was an in-joke between the three of us, she smiled.

A thought occurred to me and I laughed. 'Listen,' I said, 'no wonder they got such a fright that time when we were trying to work out who was on board.'

'Why?' asked Jamie.

'Because I said "U2", remember? They must have thought I meant "you two".'

'I hope they have to pay a hefty fine,' said Leo. 'Wasn't it quick of Pete and Tim getting the coastguard to nick them before they could go far. What do you think they'll be charged with, Mr Stephenson?'

'Menacing with a weapon, for one thing,' said Mr Stephenson. 'And theft of an inflatable and outboard motor for another.'

'And what about the book? Will they be charged over that?' continued Leo.

Mr Stephenson shook his head. 'Shouldn't think so,' he said.

'They didn't have it in their possession,' put in Mrs Stephenson.

'But Don Pedro stole it,' persisted Leo.

Mrs Stephenson laughed. 'Leo, they could hardly be charged for something an ancestor did hundreds of years ago.'

Leo leaned forward in his seat, almost breathing down Mr Stephenson's neck. 'I wish they could,' he said. 'I wish they could be thrown into the nick for ages.'

Jamie nudged me. 'What made you think that Carla and Pedro knew it was a book all the time?' he asked.

Mrs Stephenson leaned back again and looked at me. At first I was defensive, thinking she was going to make some put-down remark. But I realised she was genuinely interested, so I put my paranoia on hold.

'Something Pedro said,' I replied. 'That time Carla and Leo and I came back after hiding the book. Leo shouted out that we'd found it. Nobody had said anything about a book, but Pedro said, "*You've found the book!*" Do you remember that? You were standing on the shore with him.'

Jamie shook his head. 'No,' he said.

'Well,' I continued, 'that's what he said. It went into my mind and wouldn't go away, even though I didn't know what it was that was bugging me at the time.'

Leo leaned forward, breathing down Mr Stephenson's neck again. 'Did they know the book was stolen, by Don Pedro, Mr Stephenson? That time you were in with the garda sergeant while we were making our statements in the other room, did you find out more?'

Mr Stephenson glanced in the mirror at Leo and he smiled. 'Oh, they knew full well that it had been stolen,' he said. 'When the boat was searched, Pete went along. He found the rest of the letter and brought it back. They found someone to translate it. Don Pedro actually had the nerve to say that he had "captured decorated words of great significance from Fionn Mor O'Driscoll"!'

'He boasted about conning the man who'd protected him,' I said with disgust. 'And Carla and Pedro were going to see it through, the rotten pair of scumbags. If I'd known I'd have sunk their stupid yacht and their rotten old uncle along with it.'

Mrs Stephenson was nodding. Was my language too forcible for her gentle ears? She smiled. 'You're absolutely right, Maeve. I'd have done the same.'

Jamie grinned. 'Rubbish, Mum. You'd have won your way on board to drink cocktails with the old guy. You'd have winkled an invitation to the vineyard and, before he'd known what hit him, you'd have him convinced that he needed an architect-designed extension to his house.'

Mrs Stephenson threw back her head and laughed. I glanced at Jamie and he winked at me. He was learning how to bring up parents at long last.

'What vineyard?' said Mr Stephenson. 'There was no vineyard. The youngsters' parents are dead. They've been brought up by this uncle who's a small-time crook back in Spain. The vineyard story was just a carefully planned sympathy-getter.'

'Isn't it funny how they were all called Peter?' said Leo, with his uncanny knack of bringing something completely trivial into the conversation.

'Who?' I asked.

He turned to look at me. 'Don Pedro, Pedro and Pete,' he said, numbering them on his fingers. 'All Peters.'

'All called after a rock,' I laughed. 'That figures. Rocks in their heads.'

Leo wrinkled his nose at my mocking his powerful observation and turned back to Mr Stephenson's neck.

'Will you bring us for a sail?' he asked, with that ability of the very young to get to the really important things in life.

'Leo,' laughed Mr Stephenson, 'I'll make you into a yachtsman worthy of sailing around Cape Horn.'

Mrs Stephenson looked back at me. 'And what about Maeve?' she said. 'Don't you want to learn?'

'The sea holds no fears for me,' I said proudly. 'But someone else can do the driving. Life's too short for pulling ropes and dribbling over numbers on maps.'

She bared those teeth again, but this time there was real humour in her grin. I knew we'd never shop for frocks together, but the distance between us was getting narrower.

Epilogue

The sun was really warm, but not so warm that you'd poach your face. The nice breeze blowing in from the sea made sure of that. Besides, Cordelia Lyn had given me some of her humungously expensive cream.

'It will initiate a nice tan,' she'd said, 'without letting you burn. Help yourself to it any time, Maeve.'

The voices of the other four shouting to one another didn't bother me at all. In fact their hard-working bustling made my lazing all the more restful. I let the events of the past couple of days run through my mind again. The downside of our little adventure, of course, was the nipping in the bud of my Great Romance with Pedro. I sighed and let the tragic moment wash over me.

FAREWELL TO THE SPANISH PIRATE

A Sad Poem by Maeve Morris

The lovely maiden wiped her eye
And waved her pirate king good-bye.
'You rotten creep,' she sadly bawled,
As to the nick the hunk was hauled.
'You've left me here to mope and sob.
You wretch, you prat, you thieving yob.

'Maeve,' Leo's voice cut into my lazy daydreams. 'Are you sure you don't want to know how to...'

'No thanks,' I called back. 'You folks go right ahead and splice your mainbraces, polish your barnacles or scupper your anchors. I'm totally happy to lie here and listen to the gulls.'

Mr Stephenson had offered again to teach me to sail. But I'd declined on the grounds of being sane. Only suckers would engage in all that hard work, hopping about pulling ropes and worrying about that cruddy great sheet that kept the boat in motion. No, not for me all that hassle. I was quite content to let them do all that stuff while I lay here on deck nodding off with the gentle motion. I'd conquered that great, wet, wavy mass of water. It would take a tidal wave of gigantic proportions to bring that green hue to my face ever again. My parents would pass away with the shock when they found out.

The piebald tan was beginning to even out and my face was beginning to resemble coffee cream rather than lobster.

'You're a lazy slob.'

I opened one eye and laughed as Jamie sat beside me.

'I am, and loving every slobby second of it,' I said. 'Why are you sitting here annoying me? Won't this tub sink if you don't get out there and tie some funny knots?'

'Probably,' he said. 'But you're used to the sea by now, so it won't bother you if you have to swim ashore.'

'Not a bother,' I said. 'The sea knows better than to argue with me now.'

'What about buses?' Jamie said with a chuckle.'Will you not be throwing up on buses now either?'

I sat upright and scowled at him. 'Very funny,' I said. 'Excruciatingly witty. Better stay back, sunshine, or my stomach might remember that's it's rocking about here in the open sea. Wouldn't like to spoil that nice orange life-jacket, would we?'

'Those waves are called white horses,' called Leo, pointing to where the sea was splashing against the cliffs in great white foam

I gave a very exaggerated sigh and brushed my hand across my brow. 'Try not to mention horses, Leo,' I said. 'It only serves to remind me of Pedro. He and I would have made a great couple riding our white horses through the vineyard.'

'There's no vineyard, remember?' laughed Jamie

'Wouldn't matter,' I replied. 'I still think of us riding these white horses in my fantasy.' I closed my eyes and faced the sun. I gave another deep sigh. 'Sad ending,' I continued. 'He'd such great eyes, Pedro.'

'And Carla was such a beauty,' said Jamie.

'A real looker,' added Leo.

'Steal your heart as quick as she'd look at you,' went on Jamie.

My eyes snapped open. 'Yes, well there's no need to go on about them,' I said.

Both Leo and Jamie laughed and I realised they were putting one over on me. 'Shouldn't you two sailor boys be scrubbing a deck or splicing a spinnaker or something?' I said.

'Don't worry, Maeve,' consoled Jamie. 'Carla didn't have your neck.'

My neck! At long last he noticed my long, elegant neck. My swanlike, graceful, feminine neck. I lowered my shoulders to make it look even longer. *Sometimes,* I thought, *sometimes it's good to be a woman.*

'What do you mean, Jamie?' I asked sweetly. I'd have simpered if I'd known what the word meant. Women in old books do it a lot.

'Your hard neck,' he said. 'She didn't have your hard neck and macho courage.'

Just for a moment I found myself identifying with the virago who'd stretched Labhras O'Loinseach's ears for him. Perhaps she'd had the right idea.

'You're crowding my sunshine, you two,' I said. 'I'm in an ear-stretching mood today, so run along before some barber's harp gets to sing about you.'

Jamie laughed and twisted my baseball cap back to front.

MARY ARRIGAN lives in Roscrea, County Tipperary. As well as writing books for teenagers, she has written and illustrated books in Irish for younger children.

Her awards include the Sunday Times/CWA Short Story Award 1991; The Hennessy Award 1993; a Bisto Merit Award 1994; and International Youth Library choice for White Ravens 1997.

This is her third book for The Children's Press. The other two are *Dead Monks and Shady Deals* (1995) and *Landscape with Cracked Sheep* (1996).